shadow

JUNIOR TEN

HELL'S GATE

By Erik Schubach

Lands of Spiro
Inhabitable Lands of Earth

Uninhabitable Lands

Uninhabitable Lands

Uninhabitable Lands

Uninhabitable Lands

N
E
W
S

Hell's Gate
God's Eye Lake
Blazing Desert
The Great Sea
Solomon Keep
The Great Desert
New World Keep
Serpent Tail Lake
Lake Visintine
Fae Reach Keep
Whispering Winds Range
Heaven's Gate Mountain
Defiance
Lake Irk
Peach Hollow
Lake Odette
The Grasslands
Dragontooth Lake
Westburg Keep
Gypsy Vale Lake
Iron Keep
Flachash
Cougar Peeps
Black Forest
Troth Keep
Troth Lake
The Mountith
Lake Hope
Highland Keep
The Gap

CHAPTER 1 – PACKING

I looked under my bed, where was it? After finding the scabbard for my Anadelea, empty, I cocked a brow and called out through our apartment suite in Templar Hall, "Shanicia, bring my blade back, you little sneak!"

I huffed when there was no response, and trudged out of my room and down to the first level, moving through the private kitchen, smiling at Cook, who waved a mixing spoon at me as she prepared some heavenly mouth-watering meal for us. She inclined her head with her ever-present smile. "Sora Misty."

I smiled back at the woman with her curly black tresses, which were the envy of Templar Hall, bunched up in an adorable bun. "Morning Cassidy," I said, as I entered the small dining hall that was adjacent to the entry and sitting room.

The next moment I was squeaking in horror as I watched my little sister; well she's not really little anymore as her last growth spurt left her a couple fingers taller than mom, but still much shorter than me, though I'm quite sure she'll at least equal my height when she's grown. The audacious brat was slicing pancakes with my sword!

She looked up as she took a bite of sticky, buttery, and syrupy pancake from the end of my pride and joy. Then she looked at me, innocent as you please, as she held the tip out, with a tiny piece of pancake left on it to Bitsy, our little Rockhopper. My mouth worked but no sound came out as the little rodent, with her oversize hind legs grabbed the offering off the blade with her front paws and ate it down greedily.

Mother came walking in and past us to get her morning tea from the kitchen, without slowing she kissed the top of Shanny's head, one hand deftly extricating my blade from my sis, and handed it to me as she kissed the top of my head on the way past, saying, "Use a fork like a civilized person, Shan, how many times do we have to tell you a letter opener is not a dining utensil."

I stared at my now sticky blade and gawked toward the door. "She's a proper blade, not a letter opener!" I grinned at her chuckle. Well, she was quite small for a proper sword. She, like mom's Anadele, was no larger than a parrying blade most knights used in their off hands, but she was all I needed. I preferred non-lethal weapons like staves, but Anadelea has served me well to help defend Sparo and those I loved.

At that thought, I felt the heat of her power as mom stepped into the room too, looking so much more confident than she ever has. Our misadventure to the lands of the D.C. and her epiphany there seemed to open her eyes more to the possibilities the future held for her when she will become Prime in our blended society between the Altii and the Mountain Gypsies of Sparo.

She and Mother preferred to sleep in the Gypsy Wagon out back, rather than in our apartments here in Templar Hall. It is one of the things Mom is most proud of because it is something that is hers before the title of Great Mother was forced upon her by Gramma Rain.

She was smirking slightly as her eyes virtually twinkled with the love that was almost a tangible thing she held for us. "Shan, baby girl, don't mess with your sister, and Misty, you need to hide your weapons better."

She took the time to give us each silly side-to-side hugs, then checked her gear and held her hand out as Shanny sheepishly handed back the Templar Dagger she had lifted from her. Then she winked at us. "Love you, girls," before she slipped into the kitchen with Mother. I had to smile, they still acted so much like newlyweds even after all these years.

Then I grabbed a grape from a bunch from the fruit basket on the sideboard and flicked it at my evil sister, I grinned in satisfaction as she just absently held up the fork she now had and stabbed the grape perfectly at center in the air, and then bit it off the utensil and chewed with a grin.

It was so amazing to me. I could always feel the warm glow of her life force sort of swell slightly as she did that. She was a very low-level sensitive, as many of the people out of Hell's Gate, but like most from there, would never have enough magic inside her to ignite. But even so, that swell of magic she did command, made her nigh untouchable when she held a weapon.

It tasted a little like luck, but it had an odd citrus tinge to it that told me it was a little more than that. Possibly some sort of

precision enhancement? Whatever it was, it didn't fall into the
normal Altii elemental magics, it was more akin to the magik of the
Mountain Gypsies, magik of the spirit which was more intent than
elemental manipulation. Sort of like Uncle Alexandru, whose
sensitive spark tasted almost of pure luck.

Hiding the pride I had for my little sister, I sat at my seat at the
table and started spearing some of those sinfully fluffy pancakes
with a fork onto the plate at my place setting. I took advantage of
what I knew and flicked the other grape I was palming and as she
deftly speared it, the pancake I had flung at virtually the same time
hit her full in the face to her giggling delight.

Ever since our moms fostered Shan, I've known what she could
do, and I also knew its one limitation that we still haven't shared
with even our family. She can only counter one thing at a time.

Then I shrugged and shuddered as fur tickled the back of my
neck as Itsy, our little Sugar Glider awoke and stretched, poking her
nose out from behind my hair then just leaping and gliding to the
table next to Bitsy, helping herself to the bits of pancakes Shanny
had made into a little tower there for them.

"What have we told you about your pets on the table?"

I turned sheepishly to the woman most of Sparo referred to as
the Harbinger of Wexbury or as the Mountain Gypsies called her, the
Lightbringer, though we just called her, "Yes, mother. But they're
just as bad as Shan."

She cocked an expectant brow as mom moved to her side, I

sighed and pushed just a hint of my power out, causing Mom's to flare slightly, hers reaching for mine, the little ones looked up, chittered at us as if they were chastising, then Bitsy climbed onto the bigger rodent's back and Itsy dove off the table, spreading her limbs, gliding them down to the floor and they disappeared into the mess of shredded blankets they used as a nest in the corner.

Then mom's power relaxed when I released mine. The amber and blue-tinted mists of her blended magics bleeding to white bubbling from the scars on her face. It never ceased to amaze me, and after I ignited, I've been able to feel the magic pushing from her like a cracked vessel. And though she started as a low-level magic-user... as an Adept, her power has just grown in leaps and bounds, and what leaks from her tells the story of the massive potential she still has. Though she doesn't know it, or maybe acknowledge it is the better term, her power already rivals that of myself and even Gramma Rain.

I can't imagine the ability to use all magics, I have trouble enough keeping my nature element in check. Since mine allows me to feel all the life around me, it also makes me sensitive to the emotions of those around me as it affects their lives. I still get overwhelmed in large crowds. But mom... well it has to be maddening being able to touch every kind of magic and with it, all the drawbacks each type inflicts upon the wielder. She and Mother are my heroes.

As they sat at the table, mom prompted, "Are you excited,

girls?"

I nodded emphatically. Ingr and I were escorting Shanny to her home realm of Hell's Gate in her official capacity as the commander of the Junior Regiment of Sparo. Once I became a Squire, I had to turn the title and responsibility over to her.

The Junior Regiment was officially recognized by King George, back when I was younger and he was Prince George. So that put an end to people trying to say there was no such thing as the Junior Regiment. To be fair, I had made the battalion up when I and the other children of Wexbury Keep used to play knights. But it has become something important to all the realms of Sparo. A way to teach other children that we all need to look out for those in need, or those less fortunate than ourselves.

And now that I made the mistake of making new lands with my magic to demonstrate that there is life in the Uninhabitable Lands just below the surface. Shanicia had claimed the land for Shantopia. And King George upheld her claim. I still maintain he was joking, but he'll never say if he was. He commissioned a hall to be built on the tiny, less than two-acre land plot, for the official headquarters of the Junior Regiment of Sparo, declaring it neutral ground.

And that legitimized what everyone had thought had been a royal joke. Now underprivileged commoner children are brought to... I won't call it Shantopia... the hall there to learn about the history of Sparo, and taught how to aid others in need. Uncle Bex says it's like Summer Camp. But not being born noble, I never understood what that meant.

As Commander, Shan was the ambassador for the program, and as such, the Crown has asked her to travel to each realm, to speak with the adult organizers of each region's Junior Regiment to share any new perks of the program or address any needs they have. I think it is the King and Queen's way of having fun at mom's expense.

Shan thought it would reflect poorly on the legitimacy of the program if she were accompanied by her parents, one of whom was co-ruler of Sparo. So my girl, Ingr, and I were assigned to chaperone her. Our other sister, Princess Shavon... Shanny's biological sister, Desi, wants to meet us there since it is her and Shan's home realm. I was excited to see Hell's Gate, as it is the only realm I never have visited.

And, as questionable as it may seem, sending some teens and a tween off to another realm on their own, there will be plenty of adults present to make sure nothing untoward befalls us. Unfortunately, being Sora to the Great Mother means we will never be alone or have privacy again. Royal guards from the Crown are assigned to us, and Mountain Gypsy Garda Personalas are assigned to us as well.

So between our guards, Ingr's guards, and the surely ten or twelve... even though they tell her it is only two, guards that Princess Shavon has with her, we'll have virtually a whole compliment of babysitters... I mean trained guards standing watch over us.

Shanny and I had to whine quite profusely to make our moms stay home, and before they could do it, insisted not to send Grandma or Gramma Rain with us. They reluctantly agreed. I was so excited because this would be our first time away from home, relatively as alone as we could possibly get considering.

Mom said as she sat, mother holding her chair for her, "I see you decided to go in your capacity as Junior Templar, Mist?"

I looked down to my brown and burgundy hybrid armor that was a cross between Mountain Gypsy leathers with hidden body armor plates capable of stopping a small gun weapon from Avalon, or even most blades and arrows. The only difference between it and the armor I wore as Sora of the Great Mother of Sparo, was that it wasn't brown and green with the two distinctive stripes of light green piping.

Nodding I shared, "I figured that since we are traveling for Junior Regiment business, I should wear this as it more represents the Altii side of our family."

Mother sat and nodded approval of my choice, then smirked as she said, "And in your capacity, as George's made up Junior Templar, you'll have total autonomy, and not even the Duke of Hell's Gate will have dominion over you." Caught. I tried not to smile, but she reminded me, "But as Sora of the Great Mother, you outrank him anyway."

I pointed out, with a smile on my face. "True, but then it looks as if I am hiding behind the skirt of my mother, whereas I earned my Junior Templar title through my own merits."

The title of Templar was given to heroes of the realm by the Crown, and that honor made them beholden to no man nor woman, and nobody had say nor sway over them. Templars were autonomous and looked upon as neutral parties in everything, and could command the knights of any realm.

My moms, and Uncle Bexington, through their incredible feats of bravery and honor in saving the lands of Sparo, were awarded the title. Prince George at that time had bestowed the title of Junior Templar on me. Just about everyone thinks he was joking about it, but every time he is pressed on the subject he always chuckles and asked, "As ruler of Sparo, my word is law is it not?" The argument was put to bed when I was given a Templar's dagger, a symbol of my position, and when displayed to Knights or nobles of any realm in Sparo, they are to treat my words as if the King himself had uttered them.

Mom asked as her hand blurred forward, leaving wispy ghost-like afterimages as she stuttered through time... at least that's what it has felt like to me since I ignited, and she grabbed a strip of bacon off of a plate to munch on, "Did you..."

I sighed. "Yes mom, I packed my Squire armor and my Sora armor just in case I need to assume one of my other roles. I wouldn't forget."

"She forgot, Ingr had to remind her... twice," Shan shared with a sly grin.

"Hey, you little rat! What did I ever do to you?"

"Sorry, I just think it's cute how much she dotes over you. When I grow up I hope I find someone to dote over me like that."

Ok fine, she was cute. "Half the kids in your lessons are all doe-eyed over you, sis." It was fun to see her dark skin darken more as she blushed.

Cook Cassidy came in to sit with us, setting a tray with scrambled eggs and sausage links in the center of the table. She was family and mom insisted she eats with us. "Misty, don't tease your sister, and Shanicia, you don't have to embarrass your sister. Now eat before it gets cold everyone."

Our moms chimed out with humor in their tones, "Yes Cassidy." It was evident who ran the place and it wasn't any of us. Cassidy was one of the most competent staff any family could be blessed with. Other nobles would balk at how our cook slash chambermaid spoke so informally and familiarly with us. But our family, except for Gran Margaret, were all born commoners like Cassidy, and none of us will ever forget how Nobles treated us. We would not treat anyone who worked for us as less than equals, and we will never employ indentured servants, and we pay our workers well compared to most every other noble household. And as I said, Cass is one of our family to us.

Mom turned to mother. "Love, I think at least you should..."

"Moooom! I'm a Squire, about to be wed, I think I can go on a short trip with my sister without being escorted by our parents. It's bad enough she..." I nudged my fork toward the cross timbers of the gabled ceiling. "is going to be with us, as well as all the other guards. What could possibly happen?"

She didn't even look up and tossed an apple up, and we heard the woman hiding in the shadows there take a bite of the fruit. "Your Aunt Sara is just doing her job as your Garda Personala. I had to suffer through years of Alexandru shadowing me and your mother... now there's a small army taking the last of our privacy away everywhere we go. So as your Grandma Rain says..."

Shanny and I droned out, "Suck it up, buttercup."

Mother snorted and I pointed at them. "You know we'll call your bluff one day. I've never actually heard her utter that phrase, and I may ask her. It doesn't sound like anything the People would say."

Mother Luna, how frustrating is it when your parents shoot you matching shit-eating grins with a hint of a dare in them?

We ate as we discussed goings-on in the Dig, the excavation of the settlement of Cedar Ridge from the Before Times. When the Great Wizards of the Before had amazing advanced cities and technology. Mom had discovered it back when she was a commoner, a Herder from the nearby Wexbury Keep, where she would sell the amazing things from the past, from before the moon was torn asunder by a rogue celestial body that left Mother Luna in three pieces and the Earth half-destroyed in what our scholars at Castle Wexbury call an extinction-level event.

Cassidy pointed out, "Templar Bexington is preparing for a test of his voice flash technology."

"They're called phonys, we saw them in Avalon and Uncle Bex has been trying to duplicate them ever since." Shan corrected.

Avalon is a realm that still has access to so much of the technology from the Before Times, which they used to enslave and strip the resources from the other lands they scouted in the Uninhabitable Lands. They had taken over three peaceful lands before they dared pick a fight with Sparo, the first people of what they called the Outlands who knew how to wage war and possessed magic like the Wizards of the Before must have wielded. But Avalon didn't know how to fight against something they didn't understand or possess.

The knights and magic users of Sparo had dealt them a decisive defeat and now occupy their frozen land in the north to make sure their military doesn't rise up again to wage war on other lands.

Years ago, Bex had created a means in which we could communicate between the realms, keeps, and castles using wires strung between all the lands that were hooked up to lights with letters on them, the whole system powered by paddle wheel generators in rivers and magic spark vessels where free electricity was not to be found. We called the messages flashes since it was a series of flashing lights.

But now, the man who always has his mind in the sky, developing genius ideas to bring us to parity with the last age of mankind, thinks he has figured out how to duplicate the voice-over electricity technology we witnessed in Avalon.

The "Purists" in Avalon, a radicalized terror group who believes Avalon was in the right to enslave the Outlands and is trying to get Sparo to withdraw from Avalon, think we are stealing their technology. However, that is one of the things mother has made King George promise, that we would not commandeer any technologies that the government of Avalon does not share freely with us.

And I actually think that President Esmeralda Cutter of Avalon would freely share this particular technology, but she, like us, is fascinated with the ingenuity and brilliance of our Bexington and just wants to see if he can actually do it on his own.

I, for one, know for a fact that Uncle Bex can do it. I mean, he's developed the technology over the past decade as I have grown up, that has changed the world as we know it. With Flashes, and Auto-Wagons, and Airships, and a myriad of other ingenious inventions. So this... is simply inevitable to me, and his children, the twins, have the potential to outshine him by the time they hit the age of majority as they are soaking up all he knows like little sponges and have already started developing experiments on their own.

Mom corrected Shanny before I could. "The technology is called telephony, not phonys, and the terminals themselves are called Telephones or simply phones according to Esme." Then she smirked and gave voice to my suspicions. "And the look on her face when I discussed Bex's upcoming attempt has the evil woman smirking. I swear she would have just let us have one of the devices for our brainy Templar to reverse engineer, but she's curious if he can accomplish the feat without one."

I imagined how our new streamlined Flash communications have given us almost real-time communications between realms now instead of signal fires or swift courier horses. And being able to actually speak between keeps or other Outland realms, even Avalon, will be exponentially more efficient.

I realized our moms were postponing our departure with all this talk, the sneaky women, and I was about to call them on it. We needed to get underway if we wanted to make the journey in two days to the farthest possible point in the Lower Ten realms from Wexbury. The dirigible of the Great Mother, the Jewel would have to fly at only three quarters her normal speed since we would be trailed by another dirigible airship that would carry our security detachment, much to our chagrin.

I opened my mouth to call them on it when I almost fell out of my chair I had spun so fast to the feel of a power I savored over all others as my girl glided into the room, her Gypsy skirts hanging almost to the flagstone floor, her midnight black curls pooling on and over her shoulders framing her olive complexioned skin. Her magik and presence and life always glowed in my vision and my heart actually skipped a beat at her smile.

She said in the tongue of the People, affecting a no-nonsense tone I've heard her mother, Sylvia, used on many an occasion, "Mist, Shanny, everyone is waiting on you at the landing pads. Chop chop, we must depart or we'll be a day late." Then she curtsied. "Great Mother, Sora Celeste."

Mom huffed in the same tongue as she stood to her full five foot nothing, even though she tells everyone five foot one, and opened her arms expectantly. "You'll not get away with that Great Mother nonsense soon, lady, you'll have to call me mom in a short while."

Ingr hugged mom then reached out a hand causing mother to sigh and grasp her fingers lovingly. Heaven forbid the Harbinger of Wexbury show emotion. She knew she didn't have to affect her stoic looming presence around family, we knew the real her, the insecure Trapper girl who became the most feared Knight in all the realms to those who would do the innocent harm.

Mother said, "I guess we can't stall the girls anymore, love." Then she turned to me and Shan who was collecting Itsy and Bitsy. "Are you sure you don't want us to come along? We can make it a family holiday." But what I really heard was we're scared to let you two out of our sight, what with Avalon Purists, and traitors loyal to the Rogue Duchess Aelwen still in hiding in Sparo. Not to mention rogues and marauders.

I absently rubbed my forehead at the thought of that psychotic Aelwen, as phantom remembered pain from headbutting her and breaking her nose... twice, manifested. "I'm a Squire and Junior Templar moms, we're just going to another keep and there is plenty of security there and unfortunately coming with us. Why don't you get this overprotective when we go alone to Highland to visit Shavon?"

Mom said for her, "Because you have the full protection of the Crown and the royal guards at the capitol, sweetie." Her smile was too cute and loving for the most dangerous person on the face of the earth. But that's what made her, well, her. The love was her, completely, and she feared and dreaded the power she kept locked away but was forced time after time to unleash when defending the defenseless or the people she loves.

I sighed heavily and asked, "Fine, you can see us off so long as you don't embarrass us in front of everyone in Templarville."

She grumped. "I'm never calling it that."

And they followed us out to the waiting airships as Shanicia and I donned our cloaks to fight the chill of the fall air. We blurred slightly like mom, but not because we were time splitting like her, but because all the Touched of the People had imbued our cloaks with hundreds, if not thousands of charms like luck, or keeping us at a comfortable temperature despite the weather, and the incredible weight of the magic caused the blurring effect. It always made me blush when the Gypsy half of our family doted on us like that. I felt honored and blessed.

Ingr had my hand in hers and Shan's in her other as we made our way through the crowd gathering at the airships on the stone anchoring pads that were added to Templar Hall's courtyard, then I sighed heavily again and shot an accusing look back at our smug-looking moms.

The flanking vessel for the trip was none other than the latest version of the Outrider. The sneaky women. Since they couldn't come, they were sending Uncle Bex with us. He let nobody but, well but my family fly his Outrider. They were sending a full Templar to watch over our little excursion. Subtle.

They had no shame as they shrugged. We noted Grammy Margret, Gramma Rain, and Aunt Sylvia by the ramp into the Jewel to see us off as they shooed the porters who had moved our things into the vessel. We hugged our moms, then hustled to hug our grams and Sylvia goodbye. I called out as Aunt Sara pulled the ramp which doubled as the door up in place, "Love you all, see you in a few days."

Then both Shan and I came to a halt as we tried to beat each other to the airship's controls, just to find Aunt Sara had beat us to them. "Hey! No fair."

"Oh hush, Soras, just relax and maybe I'll let one of you fly a little later."

Shan prompted with guile, "We both outrank you, Auntie."

"Yes, but your mothers outrank you, and already gave me instructions."

Ok, I had to chuckle at that. Of course, they did. So I shrugged and stated the obvious since it was where we were overnighting, "Next stop, Solomon Keep."

CHAPTER 2 – HELL'S GATE

That's how we found ourselves the following evening as Father Sol touched the horizon, approaching the lights of Hell's Gate Keep by God's Eye Lake, the only body of water in the realm that was covered by the Burning Desert.

I had to chuckle at the memory of the prior night. Duke Liam and his blushing bride, Duchess Ariel of the Aratraya band of Mountain Gypsies had gone out of their way to throw a big banquet for us and Shavon, who appeared almost simultaneously at Solomon Keep as we arrived. We gave way to the small flotilla of heavily armored airships escorting the new crowned jewel and namesake of the Highland fleet.

It made me feel a little better that we only had to contend with one airship full of protectors, poor Shavon had an entire battalion of royal guards, and even Gypsy Garda Personalas to honor our new dually ruled society, to protect her. For as overprotective I felt our moms were, King George and Queen Everly were orders of magnitude more protective of their fostered daughter... the Crowned Princess and heir to the throne.

Once Shavon and no less than three dozen guards disembarked and the airships moved to holding hangars by the huge airfield constructed next to Solomon Keep, we landed in our much smaller and more nimble vessels.

It was too cute to watch my little sis as she actually squealed as she dashed over to hug her sister. I still find it amazing that after their separation so very long ago, that chance and fate brought them back together again. I had rolled my eyes at the royal guards who had looked antsy as Ingr had joined me in approaching their charge. Always one for decorum and protocol, my girl curtsied Shavon before we embraced her since she was the only one of us who held a lesser rank than the Crowned Princess. Shanny and I were her peers.

Desi... Shavon, had rolled her eyes and slapped Ingr's shoulder and spoke in broken Gypsy that she was learning, "Come on lady, we're going to be sisters once you and Mist marry. Don't you think we can get past this bowing foolishness?"

I smirked as Ingr chastised her in English, sounding like her mother, "Until such time, I will maintain proper protocol..." Then she added with a smirk, "...brat."

A dozen heavily armed men in the colors of the King's own gasped and placed their hands on the pommels of their blades until Shavon chuckled and hugged Ingr, telling me over her shoulder, "This one's a keeper, Mist."

I stopped giving the overzealous guards the evil eye and smiled back at her. "Yes, she is."

Then the ebony-skinned princess looked around and exhaled in exasperation. "I gave her leave to speak plainly around me ages ago, and you lot know it."

Liam and Ariel broke the tension as they stepped up to the line of guards. Sheesh, with ours in the mix, it was a small army there on Solomon soil. The boisterous bear of a man, after bowing and being disarmed, approached.

I had to hide a smile watching the Altii guards all looking nervous and tense at the thin, long blade on Duchess Ariel's hip. But as a Mountain Gypsy woman who had taken up a blade to defend the People, was a Femeie de Sabie, a woman of the blade of the Mountain Gypsies, and it would be an insult to not just her, but to everyone around her if she were to be seen in public without her blade.

It was the same with my family since being the daughters of the Great Mother of Sparo, we were by default Mountain Gypsy Soras and Femeie de Sabies ourselves.

Liam was always such a fun man to be around because he was an honorable man who was also always looking for angles to bring his realm even more prestige than having the Great Sea in it. And it was so much more fun to watch Ariel keep him in check. She was such a slight woman, just a little bigger than mom, but she had such a commanding presence, and like Aunt Verna, had a large scar on her cheek. She had received it in battle during the Great Avalon War. It just made her look that much more intriguing.

During the entire banquet, Liam kept trying to get Shavon and me to approach our respective parents to suggest trade alliances that would favor Solomon. It wasn't until we had shut him down five or six times that a thoroughly amused Ariel chuckled. "Simply shameless, love. Leave the girls alone, they're obviously wise to you and your ways. Just allow them to enjoy the meal."

Then she turned to me. "Can you regale us of any stories of Great Mother Laney's various adventures? By all accounts, you've the heart of a bard or minstrel."

I grinned, knowing the story she wanted Liam to hear, because I had told her of mom's first hunting misadventure the last time she visited Wexbury, and I had her giggling at the part where mom dove over the log to get a turkey after she denied the other hunters a kill to allow a cougar to take down the deer Lord Peter was targeting with an arrow.

And Liam was roaring in boisterous laughter as I shared what mom had said to the bewildered men on that hunt, "This buck is hers, I will not steal from the mouth of another."

He chuckled and as he regained his composure, he said, "Your mother is always one surprise after the other."

Now here we were, only a day later, after flying over the seemingly endless expanse of the Burning Desert to arrive in the only realm I have not been to. When I was a child, before auto-wagons and dirigible airships it took the better part of a month to travel from Wexbury Keep to Hell's Gate Keep, now with these modern wonders, we can do it in two days.

After passing over the lush forests of Solomon, and crossing over the Barrier Range, the seemingly endless desert and dunes passing below us were deceiving. I could feel all the plant and animal life that seemed to subsume the last settled realm of the Lower Ten. The ten realms across the Gap of Uninhabitable Lands that Highland Reach had found so many centuries ago.

Shanny pointed out caravans of men and women below in the desert, riding the small but swift offshoots of Mustangs that have adapted for desert life, and supply wagons pulled by an unusually small oxen breed that has developed a hump on their necks to store moisture.

I noted her apprehension upon seeing the Keep as we approached God's Eye Lake. I knew it was because the people who bought her from the marauders who killed her birth parents lived in the Keep. But it was quite expansive, so the odds we would catch sight of them was slim, and our guards wouldn't allow them within a hundred yards of her anyway.

I had to blink at the sight before us. Even with twilight slowly swallowing the colorful red and orange fire in the sky of a desert sunset, I could see the wonder that was Hell's Gate proper. Wexbury was one of the smaller realms by population, but we had twenty-three settlements... twenty-four if you counted Templarville. But Hell's Gate had but two. Their namesake where the Keep resided, and the small settlement at the Zarmin Oasis which was halfway to the Barrier Range.

Hell's Gate proper stretched almost a hundred miles along the River Styx between God's Eye and Last Hope, the tiny, glacier-capped range that marked the end of the habitable lands. Virtually the only perpetual source of fresh water for the entire realm except for Zarmin. There were also three or four other oases that dotted the realm, tiny, which dried up in mid-summer.

But that band of lush life, a green valley that defied the encroaching sands, filled with life, held ninety percent of the population of their realm, over one hundred and five thousand people called Hell's Gate proper their home.

It was my turn to point to the dunes, maybe five miles out into the desert, where they looked to be cultivating a crop in a green space in the sands, with what looked to be a sea of colorful silk fabric sheets in long pickets along the rows of grain.

"That fabric stretched out there on those posts captures the moisture in the air when the cool air of the night is warmed in the morning by Father Sol, the dew condensate drips off the fabric to supply water where there normally isn't any. Uncle Bex pioneered that technology when he was on the Far Reach mission with our moms." I told my sister.

She nodded slowly and whispered, "The Monolith..." I nodded back, suppressing a shudder. We knew the true story of what had occurred on that ill-fated mission, not the one all the Knights involved swore to about Lord Samuel being the hero of the Monolith before he died. Our moms told us what had really occurred, but it is a secret even now that everyone knows that mom is an Adept.

I noted the oppressive heat of the realm was already cooling on my uncovered hands, though it was nothing compared to the heat of

New Cali, even still, I was glad for the thermal comfort my spelled cloak afforded me.

As we slowed and dropped to a hundred feet above the lake, following the approach lane Shavon's airships were taking to the Keep, I reached out to touch the environment around us. I could taste the life in the desert behind us and the much more intense life ahead of us, but I noted something interesting.

Where there is water, there is life, and I could feel hundreds of feet under the sand, huge reservoirs of plant life. Smiling I realized that Hell's Gate was like so much of the rest of the Lower Ten, with the oceans which once covered most of the planet now below the shattered and sometimes flipped tectonic plates. The tiny plants called plankton, and lichen infested the salty waters far below, and I could feel that life.

I wondered if one day those oceans would once again make their way to the surface, waking up the world again, swallowing the Uninhabitable Lands, and returning us to the blue marble I have seen in the scrolls and tomes in the Penny Library back home. But our scholars say it will be tens of thousands of years, if not millions before the dark side of the Earth cools down enough to negate the expansion caused by the Great Impact. When the crust contracts again, the water will basically be squeezed back out to the surface, though a huge amount of it was vaporized on impact.

When Sara said, "Girls, get back from the windows," I looked to where her sharp eyes were scanning. I nodded, seeing the bright red sails on the armored and armed Hell's Gate dirigibles that seemed to ring the Keep.

Most of the realms concentrated on armored troop transports with the limits of lift envelope space the Crown allowed each realm for their own self-defense. But Wexbury and Hell's Gate went a different direction. Instead of the massive vessels, the others opted for, we went with small, swift agile vessels. So instead of three to five airships, Wexbury had almost two dozen smaller ships that could swarm to overpower or outrun any other vessels.

Until proper swift courier vessels were constructed, the Crown and everyone else relied upon Wexbury to play courier or to transport small groups of people to important gatherings or meetings.

And Hell's Gate? They have fourteen of what they call Sky Sails. Smaller vessels like Wexbury, only more heavily armored. And to make up for the loss of speed caused by the extra mass, they outfitted their dirigibles with sails like on water vessels, to allow the wind to assist their airships to come close to matching Wexbury speeds if the winds favor them. They were spectacular to look at, almost works of art, but at the same time a little unnerving. We could see the ballista ports open on them as they tracked our procession through the sky.

The giant harpoons they shot had barbed blades made of the magnesium they mined from Last Hope. And they would ignite the magnesium as they launched them from their vessels. And magnesium burns hot enough to melt through even the armor on Avalon tank vehicles, so imagine what it can do to even an armored gondola, or heaven forbid, the lift envelope of a rival airship.

Shan stopped to take one last look before moving to the controls with me and Sara. The reticence in her expression had changed to one of excitement as we started to land at a huge landing complex that was in an area that was contained within an extension of the Keep's walls. I noted four barracks lined up adjacent to the wall,

Note to self, don't mess with Hell's Gate, their Knights are some of the most durable and formidable among the Lower Ten. Their keep has never fallen to a rival army since their realm was founded, and that was saying something because six of the others have been overrun many times in their history.

I grinned in pride knowing that Wexbury, small as we are, has never been breached either.

I've heard the bards' songs about Hell's Gate, and have seen many renderings on scrolls and in tomes of its keep, and even more recently, some of those new pictures made by the ancient technology called photography. It really isn't a lost technology since Avalon still used it even after the world burned. But reading the concept behind it in the tomes of the Penny Library, it has been recreated by our scholars in recent years.

The photographs do not do the majesty of the keep justice. The massive stone walls are twice the height and girth of those of my home realm, carved from a sedimentary stone in quarries in the foothills of Last Hope, and polished to a shining finish. The stone masons who had constructed the walls had done such precision work that it was extremely hard for me to pick out the seams of each of the staggeringly large stones in the smooth surface of the barrier which has never been breached by the groups of sand marauders, or the other realms like New World and Defiance in the past.

As we lowered behind these protective walls that had multiple armed sentries patrolling them, I just stared in shock and awe of the Castle in the center of the keep. It looked like something right out of the stories of castles and knights we heard as children. Wexbury's castle is pretty utilitarian, with just a few towers but has nothing really noteworthy about it. It is all the other things in the keep that has people come from all the other realms just to see or experience, like the public bath house, the Cathedral we all just call the Church, and the Great Library of Wexbury that had been second only to the Royal Library in Highland Reach... until the Public Library of Cedar Ridge... the Penny Library had been unearthed.

This castle rivaled Highland Castle. Spires and towers that reached for the sky, architecture that made it more a work of ancient art than one of utility. They all glittered in silver, painted with pigments made with the worthless metal that was prevalent in the Whispering Walls and Father Stone, Kellumite. The grainy mess of a metal that crumbled with any sort of pressure, the metallurgists can't combine it with other metals to make alloys. And it was barely workable because of its instability, so gaudy jewelry, and trinkets are all it is good for except for the sparkling and glittering silver effect it gives to paints, which never dulled because it doesn't oxidize like many metals.

They must have imported the pigments from the realms bordering the Whispering Walls, like Wexbury, since Kellumite was the one metal not found in the Last Hope range.

The overall effect on the awe-inspiring structure was a grand statement, to illustrate that though they had been the most isolated keep in Sparo until the Outlands had been found, but that they rivaled the other realms, including Solomon in almost every way.

As we touched down, we could see the huge arched building where their airships moored between missions, and all the maintenance to keep the complex vessels running was performed. Uncle Bex calls such structures hangars. A courier vessel was in one of them getting its lift envelope replaced.

They certainly took their dirigible fleet seriously. This is understandable, since in a new era where attacks no longer come from just the ground, but from above, it was prudent to maintain your air defense.

I squinted, finding it oddly... empty except for the mechanics we saw working in the hangar. They must have sent everyone away for our arrival. There were just two large men and a tall woman in the colors of Hell's Gate waiting a hundred feet beyond where Princess Shavon's vessels set down. The people of most realms, including ours, and even the Mountain Gypsies turn out in droves to see visiting dignitaries.

This was yet another example of how their isolation has created an almost separate culture here. But now that it doesn't take weeks or months to travel to the other realms, we hope to bridge the gap between us all, but not lose the unique cultures of any of the realms in the process. It is the variety of cultures that makes Sparo strong and stops us from becoming a totalitarian or oppressive people as Avalon had become.

We waited as we powered down watching all the guards flow out of the escort vessels... including ours, and they sort of assembled into three distinct layers that made me grin. The Crown's Own, the Templar's Own, and the Gypsy contingent minus Sarafine.

Uncle Bex stopped beside the Jewel to wait for us to disembark. I cocked my head, he still looked a little awkward in the way he seemed distracted by everything, but I have seen him become a formidable Knight and Templar as I have grown up, and he has the Fire of Wexbury in his heart.

Once we saw Shavon step out of the Highland, we dropped our door ramp and joined Bexington. He always had a goofy smile on his face for us. And Shanny absently took the wiry man's hand then mine and dragged us toward where the three figures were taking a knee in front of Desi. "Come on, come on." Then she looked over to my girl who looked thoroughly amused by her antics. "Ingr, tell my wretch of a sister to hurry."

It was all I could do to stop from stumbling as I got weak in the knees at the smile the Sora of my heart shot me, mischief twinkling in her eyes. "You heard my future sister, love, hurry up now." She winked then started to tickle Shan who let go of me and escaped to hide behind Bex as she squealed.

I looked at my pseudo-uncle and exhaled in exasperation, "Children."

He always seemed to look at all of us with pride in his overly intelligent eyes as he informed me as he held a hand at waist level, "I can remember a tiny little girl who knew no fear and took on even the Crown's Own with nothing but a stick."

I rolled my eyes at the teasing man as he gave me a one-armed hug as we walked to catch up with Shavon. As soon as we arrived, Ingr stood behind us and to our left, but Shan, myself, and Bex all standing even with Shavon as her peers or those who stood outside of the rule of the realms, then the two men and the woman looked us all over. And the older of the two men, who had to be as big as Tennison back home, at least six foot four, and all muscle, seemed to fixate on me for a moment before turning to the others with him.

Their stark white light robes that were marked with the colors of their realm, were a stark contrast to their dark ebony skin that was even darker than Shanicia's and Shavon's. I noted empty scabbards on both men's backs and just a cursory look at the statuesque middle-aged woman and the way she held herself and moved told me that the thin empty scabbard on her hip wasn't the only weapon she carried on her person. My mother is one of the deadliest predators in Sparo, known as the Harbinger of Wexbury, so I recognized another apex predator when I saw one.

The seals on the scabbards told the rest of the story if the taste of magic hadn't already clued me in. The man and woman were Duke Rojah and Duchess Aisha. Though Hell's Gate had a disproportionately large number of low-level sensitives who barely held a spark at all, it was extremely rare for the people of Hell's Gate to ever ignite to become full-fledged Techromancers. All the Dukes and Duchesses of the Lower Ten had always hidden that they were all Techromancers as well.

So knowing this, and that they only had seven full magic users in all their realm, it was simple to deduce before we were even introduced. The younger man, I didn't know, but I tasted no magic from him though his curiosity was so intense I had to lock down my empathy because it was so loud.

The Duke took a knee and smirked to himself as he said while the other two followed suit. "Sora Shanicia, Sora Ingr, Templar Bexington..." Then he looked at me. "And we were told what to look for from the Bane of Avalon to know in which capacity you were enjoining us with, Junior Templar Misty." What? The Bane of Avalon?

The younger man said behind his breath, though I caught it, "There's no such title."

With a speed that belied his age, the older man's hand shot out to slap the back of the other's head. "Hani, curb your tongue, the word

of the Crown or the Great Mother is law. There may well have
never been such a title as Junior Templar in the past, but the King
has decreed it so it is so."

I blinked as I realized this was the son of the Duke and Duchess,
Marquess Hani, but he was only two years my senior and he was
such an imposing figure? And... I looked from him to Ingr then
back... I didn't like that his attention was on her as his father went
on. "Welcome to our humble realm. The representatives from the
Hell's Gate Junior Regiment are all abuzz about their commander
coming to speak with them." He inclined his head to Shan.

I liked the man already, he was quick on the uptake, seeing
which armor I wore and the Templar dagger on my belt, so he
addressed the two who outranked him first, Shan and Ingr. If I had
been in my role as Sora, I would have been addressed first.

Shan grinned at me, almost like a "so there" look. Then said
almost regally, "It is good to be home again, I look forward to
speaking with you and them about the exciting new developments
for the program."

Shavon cocked an eyebrow, impressed at her little sister's ability
to turn off the jokester personality that was her default, and suddenly
sound cultured, educated, and professional like this. Then she hip-
checked her slightly to remind her about humility. Shan added,
"The Keep is as beautiful as I remember, you do the realm proud."

I caught the slightest nudge of Shavon's chin, Damn, she was
getting good at that, and the Duke and the others stood back up. The

man's arm reached forward and stopped when the sounds of blades being half-drawn all around us were heard. I sighed in exasperation, the man had no weapons and it was his keep. Overprotective louts.

He just twisted his hand to show it was empty, then cautiously reached forward again, to clasp forearms with Bex. "I take it the girls are your charges in..."

Uncle Bex snorted, holding up a halting hand as he shared, "Twould be easier to contain a tornado. No, Rojah, I'm just transport for the girls as a favor to the Great Mother." It took Bex years to stop addressing those who used to outrank him by their titles and use their given names instead since he stood above all as Templar, so every man, woman, and child, no matter their rank or standing, commoner or noble, was his peer. So I was happy to see that he has grown into his new role finally. "Shanicia is heading up this visit."

The three seemed to digest this then the Duke seemed to shake his head clear and said, "As you have surmised, I am Duke Rojah and this is my wife and enforcer of the Hell's Gate Brigade, Duchess Aisha, and our son Marquess Hani." He added for some reason, "He's of marrying age and is as of yet unattached, good stock, though no spark."

Oh, wait... my eyes widened in understanding and I cleared my throat gently and grasped Ingr's hand, and she laced fingers with me. Hani's eyes moved from her to our hands. That's right, pretty boy, she's taken... move along. Mother Luna, was I jealous?

I understood their thinking, it was getting to be sort of a problem with nobles since we became a dual governance people, their chances of their families rising in noble rank to be contenders to the throne if the Crown had no heirs was unlikely. But now there was a second path open to them, as the rank of the Mothers of each Mountain Gypsy family equated to royalty, that made their daughters, their Soras, the equivalent of princesses. So if they could marry their children into Gypsy families by their sons marrying a Sora, that would elevate them to royalty. It was all a power grab.

Mom has been working with King George about curtailing it as it has become a growing problem as the various clan Mother's have been getting approached frequently about their Soras and arranged marriages with Altii nobles. There were very few nobles who were not in it for more power, like Duke Liam. Ariel is not a Sora, so he gained no stature with his marriage, he was just truly smitten by the hard-as-nails woman who stood at his side in various battles against Avalon on the Fringe.

And here, Rojah deflated a little, Aisha looked disappointed, and her husband said as he waved it off, "Well, just consider it. With the new dual culture governance, some Mountain Gypsy blood would..." He trailed off when Ingr's grip on my hand visibly tightened.

And then all the pleasantries and scheduling began as they led us to the bustling castle. My girl breaking the awkward tension by sharing mom's idea of forming another band of the People to inhabit the small Last Hope range so that Hell's Gate had Mountain Gypsy representation like all the other realms.

She had this way of putting everyone at ease. As we passed by one of the ten soaring portcullises of the keep, I got a sick feeling in my gut, as I felt something was not right with the browning vegetation in the ornate arches beyond the gates that led into a natural space instead of into the town outside the walls of the keep. Why did it feel so... wrong to me? Even in areas where all vegetation has died off in other lands, I didn't get this oily dead feeling about it.

Shan caught my distraction and looked out at the sickly-looking vegetation beyond the walls. I made a mental note to bring it up at the banquet being prepared for the Crowned Princess, Soras, and Templars who have come to visit their realm.

CHAPTER 3 – BAZAAR

I t was a pretty standard banquet. I still can't get used to all the food that has been made available to me since my moms fostered me. Being cobblers, our family was a little better off than most of the other commoners who lived down in Cheap Quarter or the Trough. But especially in winter, where coin and food were scarce even in Mid-End where we lived because not many people were bringing in shoes for repair, and nobles didn't buy many new shoes in the cold months.

We felt lucky to have a single meal a day of dried jerky and dried vegetables to make a soup and thanked all the gods who may be looking down upon us that Wexbury Keep hosted a feast at the castle courtyard every Holy Day where we could eat our fill once a week. And when business was booming in the warmer months, my family ate much better than most serfs.

Now, whenever I could, I went out with mom or the Junior Regiment to hand out penny vouchers to all the commoner families to assure they ate well as often as the vouchers afforded them, or they could use them to buy much-needed things for their household.

That thought made me smile at the memory of meeting my future mother the first time. The keep instructor had been giving us children a tour of the castle when we happened upon my idol. The Herder girl who became Knight of the Realm, Laney Herder, the Penny Lady of Wexbury. Her kindness was a legend among us commoners and scorned by many nobles. Whenever we played Knights, I would always be her while the other children chose Sir Tennison or Lady Celeste.

She was even prettier up close than from afar and the mists that drifted from her scars were amazing. And on her hip, the fabled blade, Anadele, who the porters on that ill-fated mission to Far Reach say was so sharp that it actually split bolts of magic lightning targeting our Duke Fredrick.

She was kind to us all even though it was apparent she was in a rush, but she took the time to speak with us, and single me out to entrust with penny vouchers to distribute to the families most in need in Cheap Quarter and the Trough. So that's when I rose to the challenge and formed the Junior Regiment to aid our Lady in her quest to bring aid to those most in need.

And I've been able to watch as the Penny Lady has defied all odds, and I take pride that a commoner like me has now risen to be co-ruler of Sparo. My mom.

That reminded me. I absently touched my coin purse on my hip, feeling the bulk of the hundreds of penny vouchers mom and I procured for this outing in Hell's Gate. I'd have to find the appropriate band of mischief makers in the village to distribute them. Shanny had a little chest containing over a thousand of them for the members of the Junior Regiment here to distribute over time as well.

"I noted the plants outside one of the portcullises were suffering from some sort of blight that didn't feel right," I asked our hosts.

Aisha and Rojah exchanged a look. The Duchess whispered to herself, "Doesn't feel...?" then she smiled at a realization. "Ah, that's right, we forgot you are a Nature Elemental." Then she started fishing. "Some say your nature spark is greater even than Lady Margret of Wexbury, recognized as the most accomplished Nature Elemental in generations."

I shrugged, affecting the same reticence to speak of my capabilities to others, the same way Mom, Mother, and Gramma Rain do. Am I just that jaded by the betrayals and war I've seen in my few short years of life that I don't like others knowing of my abilities or limitations? It is best to show just enough to garner respect, but still hold back so that opponents will underestimate you.

I said as I let a trickle of power go, "I do alright, but Lady Margret is if you will pardon the terrible pun, a force of Nature who shouldn't be discounted so." At my invisible urging, Itsy and Bitsy poked their heads out from the hood of my cloak where they had been curled in napping. They crawled down my arms and stood on the banquet table and proceeded to chitter and chastise me for waking them.

They were amused at my demonstration, and boys being boys, Hani had half stood, eyes wide in amazement and excitement at seeing the two rare animals who had just noticed that they were on a table full of foods, so lost interest in chittering their discontent with me. I tore off two tiny pieces of hard bread that had a cheesy crust and placed them in front of them.

They scooped up the offerings and I said, "Ok now, not everyone enjoys seeing rodents on their tables, tuck yourselves back away now you unrepentant mooches," and with a whisper of power, I impressed my intent on them and they skittered up my arms to disappear back into my cloak.

Hani asked, "You've tamed them. Can I see them again?"

Aisha patted the air to dampen his enthusiasm and he sat as she said, "The Junior Templar has questions, Hani dear, there will be time for pets later." Then to me, she said, a touch of worry in her tone, "The blight has been slowly spreading through Hell's Gate proper for a few weeks now, and has just reached the keep in the past couple days. Livestock and people have been getting ill as the vegetation along the river has been dying. We believe it to be seepage from our metals mining operations somehow fouling the waters."

Rojah continued, "We are trying to ascertain the contamination to contain it and didn't wish to trouble the Crown. But the source eludes us, and we have started caravans mining the glaciers themselves for fresh water for our people and livestock. We were going to send a flash to the Crown if we can't resolve the problem ourselves in the next couple weeks."

Ingr sat taller beside me. "People are sick? How many? May I see them? I am a healer of the People, maybe I can help."

The Duchess sat up taller in interest. "A healer like your

mother? I witnessed the wonder of Gypsy healing magic during the war. How did we not know the Sora of the Lupei was a healer? We knew you were of the Touched."

Rojah prompted, "Do the same types of magiks of the People run in families? Or is it random like Altii magic?"

Ingr's lip quirked in a restrained smile and exchanged an amused look with me, and she could get away with being blunt like I could not, she was too adorable to be offended by. "A fishing expedition on an offer of assistance to your people?"

They took all of a second to determine playing dumb wouldn't fly there, and they chuckled as the Duke just inclined his head slightly, accepting defeat. "You cannot blame us, all realms do the same, trying to gather as much knowledge about other realms and the People as we can. Do the Gypsies not have a saying about it?"

Ingr grinned cutely and said, "Cunoașterea este putere... knowledge is power."

Then Aisha said, hope in her tone, "We would be grateful if you could see some of our sickest nobles. We could arrange a visit to the Palace Infirmary after Hani gives you ladies a tour of the keep and the Bazaar outside the gates on the morrow."

Shavon cocked an eyebrow with her other eye narrowing slightly, it was eerily similar to how Shan did the same thing when she heard something that disquieted her. "Only nobles are affected by this blight?"

"There are quite a few serfs ill too. It seems anyone who drank from the river or the central well in the village." Hani interjected, a big smile on his face as if he were trying to gain Shavon's favor. Not too smart knowing how protective the Queen was of her daughter. Calling her a mama bear would be a huge understatement. She had just sent an entire army with her so she could have a little time alone with her biological sister and me.

Ingr pursed her lips. "Can you arrange for me to see the commoners too? Are they in the infirmary or do you have... what do you call your healing centers, Mist? Hospitals?"

The Duke and Duchess seemed caught off guard at that question. It was something I have seen over and over in most of the realms, though with all the civilian outreach programs instituted by mom and the King, it is getting less frequent that we are reminded about how nobles viewed commoners before mom and Gramma Margret shook up what used to be a clear division of classes.

And I believe there was no ill intent in Aisha's tone as she said, "Well... no. They were seen by the doctors and sent to their homes. We've not enough medicines for all." This told me they were of the generation who didn't see anything wrong with caring for your nobles first. I look forward to the day where the division of classes is a thing of the past, but I had experienced it firsthand before the changes that have swept through our realm, and others like Flatlash and Solomon took our lead. Prince George has always had progressive ideas and a unique way of ruling. And now as King, he sees merit in what Wexbury is doing and has embraced the changes to our society suggested by mom, as Great Mother of Sparo.

So this is where information and education can help open the eyes of the more hidebound nobles into seeing that serfs are the backbone that holds up the realms. Ingr said to them, "It is not our way to hold one life above another, and if I see one, I will see all."

The rulers looked at each other with thoughtful expressions, weighing my girl's words, then the Duke inclined his head. "The Sora is wise, we will make it happen, Highness. Forgive us, I'm sure you see our realm as old-fashioned. But rest assured that we are trying to adapt and adjust to these new ways of thinking. As with all things, it takes time." He smirked and chuckled. "Especially among us older curmudgeons."

Ok, I liked them. I wasn't too sure before, but it was the self-deprecation there that told me they were truly trying and it wasn't just lip service.

And that's how we found ourselves outside the walls of the keep the next morning after first meal was served to us in our quarters. An entire wing of the Palace had been cleared out for our contingent.

Mother told us about the bazaar here in Hell's Gate a time or two. We've seen the markets that dwarf the one in Wexbury Keep, like Owensdale, Solomon, and Highland, but she told us that they were to the bazaar what Dragontooth Lake was to the Great Sea. But I wasn't expecting two square miles of a marketplace that was half open-air under fabric sun shades, and inside wood or stone structures coated with brightly painted river mud or clay that seemed to absorb the heat of the day to keep the interiors cooler than the ambient temperature.

And you could get almost literally everything in this market of all markets. From relics of the Before Times that had been dug up, to even fresh fish... even living ones in amazingly crafted water-tight baskets. Food, clothing, and material vendors vying for the attention of the hundreds upon hundreds of visiting nobles wearing the colors of every realm. I even saw a few people wearing the odd clothing prevalent in Avalon, and people with the colors of New Cali. This was an amazing and exciting destination for all the realms.

Hani was a surprisingly great guide. And I could see his youth in his exuberation, his imposing size just gave the impression he was older than he was.

When I caught glances at a table that had various Mountain Gypsy water skins, some singing and resonating with the same magic imbued in our cloaks, I grabbed Ingr's hand and Shavon's to drag them up to the table. Shanny was... somewhere. She had slipped the scaled-down protective unit that only had around twelve blades to guard us all, and vanished into the crowd, a look of determination on her face.

I would have worried if I hadn't heard someone cursing in the tongue of the People a moment before I felt Sarafine's tangy magic bounding off above all the fabric sheets that were stretched between poles over the bazaar to provide shade. I'm sure if anyone in the palace was looking out over the expanse of the market, they would have seen a Gypsy woman actually bounding from post to post as she tracked my errant sister.

I had a feeling I knew where she was going, and I felt for Shan. It sometimes struck me as profound that I couldn't have loved her more if we were sisters by blood, and was so proud of the person she was becoming. Don't ever tell her, but I know she is going to do great things in her life as there isn't anything in this world that can stop her if she has her mind set on something.

Slipping an army of bodyguards like this is literal child's play for her. Only Aunt Sara would be able to keep up with her, and Shan knew that. But unlike the Templar and royal guards, Gypsy Garda Personalas are tasked only to protect, not to interfere with the decisions of their charges, so Shan didn't mind... besides, Sarafine Lupei was one of the most dangerous women of our band of the People, and one of her was worth any five royal guards with my sis.

I was happy to see the woman at the table was indeed one of the People, with her characteristic black flowing hair that hung in rippling curls down her back, and her darker olive skin, which told me she was likely with one of two bands that spent more time near the Great Sea, Romanov or Aratraya, and the billowy blouse and skirt in the colors of the Aratraya confirmed it to me.

Looking at Hani I asked, "Is there any way I could talk you into getting us some of those fruit drinks we passed earlier? The heat is getting to me a bit."

He inclined his head and with gusto said, "Of course. I'll be back in a flash, ladies."

"We'll be just here."

My future bride cocked an amused brow at my subterfuge, telling me she knew what I was thinking when I saw a Gypsy vendor here. My Ingr brightened when she saw the girl behind the rolling table and smirked a little as she spoke first, "Amelia? What are you doing here?"

The woman smirked right back and gave a silly bow to us. "Sora Ingr." Then her eyes widened slightly when she looked at me, and she sputtered, "Sora Misty!" Then her eyes bugged out even more, if it were possible, as she recognized the stunning young lady with us. "Princess Shavon, Highness."

I found it amusing that my girl seemed to know this woman, and the vendor knew all of us by sight. I already had a suspicion, then the Sora of my heart introduced us, "Misty, Shavon, this is the little sister of Mother Tianna of the Aratraya."

And I could see it almost instantly, the resemblance was obvious now. Tianna had been the youngest Mother of any clan of the People when my moms first met her. Younger than I am today, but she would be what, twenty-one or two now? The young woman said in Gypsy, "I'm not little, brat. I'm only a year younger than Tianna." Then she narrowed her eyes in annoyance as she asked, "Do they all need to be here? They're scaring away customers." She waved a hand around to include even the guards in civilian garb who were pretending to blend in with the crowd bustling about, telling me her eye was just as keen as her sister's were, solidifying my suspicion about why she was here.

Just as all realms kept track of each other, the Mountain Gypsies did too. Mom shared with me how Great Mother Rain had pretended to be a minstrel on their first meeting, singing in Owensdale to take measure of her before they officially met at Father Stone. And Grandpa Nicholas had been in the Roving Band who infiltrated the various keeps just to keep an eye on the Altii who lived there since the Altii was a young and foolish people.

Nicholas had made the wonderful mistake of falling for an impulsive woman in Wexbury and married her, settling in the keep to be a chicken farmer. If only he had lived to see the amazing woman his daughter would grow up to be... my mother, the Great Mother of Sparo.

I glanced around at the guards and made a flicking motion with my hand that I've witnessed King George do many times when he wished a semblance of privacy. Uncle Bex sighed and moved back with the Templar guards, and the royal guards who looked to be panicking as they seemed to just now realize Shan wasn't with us anymore, followed suit.

But it took Shavon glaring and actually growling for her guards to follow suit, leaving us a little anonymity in the crowd. Ingr seemed endlessly amused, knowing what I was doing. I prompted Amelia in low tones in Gypsy, "Anything we should know?"

She looked at Shavon nervously and I said, "She's with us, and she understands what we are saying." I added the last just so she knew I trusted Shavon completely.

She nodded and passed me and Shavon waterskins. We examined them dutifully as she spoke in low tones, "Tianna left me here after Carnival when we learned people, the vegetation, and the land were getting sick here." There would be no other reason for a Gypsy to have a merchant table in an Altii market, as the People have no need for coin, even in our new blended society. She was left here to gather information.

She got even quieter as I exchanged waterskins with another she was holding out, palming the tiny vial she had discreetly passed me with the first one. She said one word that chilled me to the bone, I actually shivered when she nudged her chin minutely toward my hand, "Purists."

Then as if that weren't bad enough, she shared, "My brother, Merrick, has been scouting the river to try to find the source of the contamination, and caught sight of some men with their purple armbands. But more troubling than spotting Avalon terrorists, two days ago, he caught sight of an armored airship to the east that was most certainly not from Hell's Gate."

I had to rein in my anger as I hissed under my breath, "Aelwen." What was the psycho disgraced Duchess doing sniffing around Hell's Gate? Was she after the rare metals they mined? They did mine more copper, the most valuable metal in Sparo, than even

Treth. But that didn't track, she was all about power. She wanted to rule again, but not just one realm, she had grander delusions. Unfortunately, she had a knack for finding like-minded people and has spies in every realm, even Wexbury. And besides that, her main focus was to take down mom, since the crazy rogue believes that mom is the reason all of her plans were foiled, again and again.

I absently rubbed my forehead at the memory of breaking her nose, twice, by headbutting her. I swear there is always a phantom ache every time I'm reminded of it.

Nodding my thanks and dropping a silver coin in her hand and clipping the finely crafted waterskin to my belt, she whispered, "Three miles upriver in a blind cove."

Shavon did the same, only with gold. Then we acted like a couple nobles who got giddy with their purchases as Ingr winked at the Gypsy watcher as she said, "Give Tianna a hug for us."

"She'll love that. She still feels overwhelmed and isolated having the title of Mother foisted upon her."

Then we were off. Shavon hugged onto my arm, laying her head on my shoulder, and just asked through her practiced royal smile, "Will Shanny be ok?"

Where Desi was sold by the marauders who killed their parents to a couple in another realm for labor, changing her name, Shan had been sold to a larcenous couple and was forced to steal for a living as a small child here in Hell's Gate. I knew Shan wanted to check on some of her friends, the ones the residents here called street rats, from that other life of hers.

"She's so much tougher than she looks. You should be asking if Hell's Gate is going to be ok with her out there. Our sister is amazing." She sighed in relief then smiled in thanks for talking her down off the ledge, then nodded her agreement.

What must it be like for them to be reunited after so long, fearing each other might be dead. Now they both have new parents, and since fate has a sense of humor, each of those new parents is co-rulers of all of Sparo.

So I pulled up my sleeve to look at the wrist clock Mother put on me before we left on this trip. It had been Grandpa Donovan's, and he gave it to her when she hit the age of majority, and she says now she hands it down to me. We had an hour before we had to meet the Duke and Duchess at the infirmary. Come on Shanicia, hurry.

We went back to touring the bazaar as soon as Hani returned with the tangy fruit juice for us. I purchased a couple trinkets from a table full of relics from the Before Time as we perused the amazing treasures all around us.

As we were looking through some fabrics at an indoor booth which I was thinking of purchasing for Aunt Verna, whose parents owned one of the largest clothier and textile concerns in Sparo... I heard a bird calling.

I looked around then whistled back. A moment later there was a hissing ticking sound. These were Gypsy animal calls used when tracking. Someone wanted me to look to the left. When I glanced over, I saw a curtained-off area and a familiar face peeking out from behind it. Shan!

She put a finger to her lips and motioned me over with her chin.

I grabbed a skirt from a table and said, "Isn't this one darling, Ingr? I'm going to try it on in the back. Why don't you and Shavon find something cute, for Hani too, and we can have a little fun doing a little impromptu fashion show."

Her eyes flicked to where Shanny vanished to and winked, then went about dragging Shavon to another table to look through garments, Hani on their heels. Then I turned and looked at the star-struck vendor and his wife, who looked moments from squeeing over the fact she had Princesses of the Altii and the People here in their shop.

I smiled and nudged my chin to the skirt, then the back curtain, and the woman nodded furtively, blurting, "Of course, Highness. There's a changing screen in the back... can I bring you some of our more popular skirts?"

I didn't correct her with my Templar title as that was the capacity I was in at the moment, but non-military nobles and commoners aren't expected to know the difference and the nuances between them. "That would be wonderful, maybe you can find something befitting my betrothed. Thank you."

She inched her way around the guards like she was scared to get too close, then dashed off to the others, oohing and ahhing at the selections they were holding up. Ingr would keep them all busy and the attention on her and Shavon while I found out why Shan hadn't just rejoined us.

Chapter 4 – Street Rats

When I got behind the curtain, I blinked. My sister was there looking sheepishly at me, which in itself hadn't surprised me, as it was her go-to look when trying to get out of trouble with our moms. It was the other three sets of eyes on me that had surprised me.

Two boys and a girl around Shan's age, all dressed in ragged clothing indicative of Hell's Gate commoners. The boys in light, billowy fabric tunics and trousers, and the girl in a robe designed to keep the punishing light and heat from Father Sol at bay. Threadbare fabrics that had been patched so many times that I doubt there was any of the original fabric left. Their slipper-like shoes were falling apart and had scraps of fabric wrapped around them to hold them to their feet.

I had to lock down my senses and concentrate on one thing when their distrust and suspicion rolled off of them in waves as their keen eyes tracked my motions. Sometimes when emotions are too intense they overwhelm me, but if I concentrate on a singular feeling in the turmoil, I can silence most of what I am assaulted with.

I was already on edge with the emotions of the hundreds of people in the market hammering at me, and these children's emotions were like a sharp needle probing my brain. So I listened to the hope and concerning love that Shan had for me. She was always a calm in the sea for me, and the little snot knew it because she used it to get me to agree with some of her more mischievous adventures at times.

This though wasn't mischief. I could feel a steely resolve behind her emotions, whatever this was was extremely important to her. "Mist, these are the other Street Rats. We grew up together, stealing for the Weavers. This is Hak, Rual, and Kes. Guys, this is my new sister, Misty. She's one of the good ones and she can help us." Then she added with the most serious tone I've ever heard her use, "You can trust her."

They were all children of the Weavers who had bought and trained Shan to steal at such an impossibly young age? These were... I swallowed. These were her brothers and sister before she was fostered to become my sister?

When a child is fostered, they become the children of the parents who foster them as if they were their parents in blood. It has long been a tradition that once a child is fostered, then all contact with their birth parents is cut off just as all their parental rights are until the child becomes the age of majority at nineteen. Then the child can choose whether or not to contact their birth parents again.

My moms broke tradition, and they allowed my birth parents and me to visit each other whenever we want. Most other nobles in the keep looked down on us for breaking with tradition. And when Shan was fostered, our moms did the same with her, until they learned the truth of it.

The Weavers weren't even her birth parents, and the

reprehensible way they raised her to be a thief... an innocent child, was sickening. And when Shanny wouldn't rob our moms when they had come to Wexbury to visit, our moms banished the Weavers from Wexbury and Shanicia's life.

She never ever speaks of the Weavers and what she had gone through, though she did mention in passing that there were other Street Rats like her, but I hadn't known they had been her siblings as well.

My blood was boiling. There had to be something we could do to stop the Weavers from victimizing these children and others like them. Mom and King George would know what to do. I looked up into the rafters of the building to see Sarafine with her emotionless mask on. It was like armor for her to suppress her emotions, but she couldn't ever stuff them down so far an empath like me wouldn't feel. And I tasted her rage and need for some sort of vengeance over those who would wrong children like this.

The children followed my gaze and were shocked to see Sara up there. Shan didn't even look. Sara was always there, and Shanny knew that she may have slipped the rest of the guards, but never our scarily dangerous Aunt and protector. We know she's not really our aunt, but we've adopted her into our family. She was part of our band, the Lupei, so at the very least, she was like some fifth cousin or something. But in our hearts, she was Aunt Sara.

I said, "A pleasure to meet you all." Then I looked at my sis and cocked a brow expectantly.

She exhaled just like mom, and it was cute as hells. I wonder if she knows just how much she emulates her. "Things have gotten worse since I left. The Weavers are mad all the time, making my... making them take more and more chances. They're even starting to talk to the sand marauders again, about other ways to make coin."

Then she leaned in and whispered as she put a hand out for Itsy and Bitsy to flow out over my shoulder and onto hers, "They're having them steal secrets from the Palace. If they get caught they'll get executed... children or not." I could feel as much as hear the desperation in her tone.

Then she stood taller and said with steel garnering no argument, "I told them we'd take them with us."

Oh, shit. Taking someone's children? They were despicable human beings who didn't deserve children, but they were still their children.

Shan growled at me. I looked at her and growled right back. She broke first, sighing again, then brought up something I, and our moms hadn't contemplated. "Mist, please. Just like me, they were bought illegally from sand raiders. None of us were legally sold by the Duke, the Crown, or our real parents. So they were never our legal parents." I hated how her eyes always darted around in fear whenever she spoke about the Weavers like they would jump out around a corner at any second and take her back away from us.

I blinked at her, and Sarafine said softly from above. "They were all kidnapped, torn from their families like Sora Shanicia.

None of their parents live. The People call these children Foundlings. Do not the Altii have a responsibility for them, and citizens of the Crown?"

It was true. Following that logic, the Weavers were actually holding these children against their will. That would get them the stockade and the dungeons. If we would have thought of that before, then the nightmare for these children would have ended years ago.

I looked over my shoulder and called out to the curtain, "Uncle Bex? Guards?"

The kids' eyes widened and they turned as if to bolt through a little stone vent in the wall, but Shan was already there, blocking their way. "No, don't run. Misty would never betray you. She's smart and knows what to do." She took a terrified-looking Kes' hand and nodded and smiled encouragingly, but I did note how she moved in front of the three, holding an arm back to shield them, and all three laid hands on her arm and shoulder. It looked like instinct to them, and my heart broke as I imagined tiny Shan, when we first met her, protecting her siblings like this from the Weavers. She's always been so fierce and strong.

People sometimes don't take Uncle Bex seriously. He's a little gangly, and absent-minded because his brilliant mind is always dreaming up things that nobody else could even fathom. To call him a genius would be an insult to just how brilliant he is. They always discount him as a Knight and Templar, but those of us who have seen his bravery and drive to protect those he loves would assuage them of that fallacy.

I've seen the man take on five marauders to try to stop Aelwen from taking me. Even outnumbered like that, he fought with the heart of a bear, and though they overwhelmed him in the end... the bastards knew they had been in a fight and tasted the steel and fire of Wexbury, some paying with their lives.

And he almost exploded through the curtain, his powered blade sparking, connected to wires and doodads on his armor, death in his eyes. The royal guards were on his heels, blades drawn. Everyone faltered when I took a step back, to shield Shan and the Street Rats.

I looked at Bex sheepishly. Maybe calling out through a curtain wasn't the best way to go about this. I scrunched my head to my shoulders. "Sorry. It isn't an emergency or anything. I'm just a little worked up and upset." Then I stood tall and said, "These children have been kidnapped, held against their will, and forced to engage in larcenous activities for years..." I grabbed the hem of my dark red hunting cloak and showed the lining.

The royal guard and the other Garda Personalas saw the two stripes of light green piping sewn into the lining and took a knee. For this, I wasn't Junior Templar Misty, I was Sora Misty, mostenitor of the Great Mother of Sparo. Heir apparent and first in line to rule for the People after Great Mother Laney.

"I am taking them into protective custody under the authority of the Crown at this time until a proper investigation can be

performed." Then I turned to one of the two guards assigned to
Hani who had crowded in and said, "You need to find and detain
Haron and Jai Weaver for questioning. Suspicion of human
trafficking, kidnapping, dealing in stolen property, and..." I inhaled
sharply and added the new information, "And probable espionage."
That last one, if true, may very well have them swinging on a
gallows, as distasteful as corporal punishment is.

The two men just looked at me blankly, one asking, "On whose
auth..."

Hani snapped out from behind them, in an angry and assertive
tone that made me respect him, as this was the first backbone we
have seen from him, and it looked good on him, "Look at her, fool.
She displays the mark of the Great Mother! Sora Misty is a royal
and we serve at her pleasure, and even if she did not feel the need to
act in that capacity, that Templar dagger at her hip gives her
authority over any Knight in any realm."

Then to add to the embarrassing looks the two knights were now
wearing, he added, "And if that is not good enough, then I,
Marquess Hani of Hell's Gate, heir of Duke Rojah, order it so." The
two snapped to attention, then bowed to me and then to Hani before
dashing back out.

That's when Shavon poked her head in with the love of my life,
as Ingr asked innocently, "So this is where everyone is, what did we
miss?"

She didn't even slow as she passed by everyone, drifting her fingers lightly along my arm, the electric tingle of our magics recognizing each other, and she slipped in front of Shan and the other children protectively. Mother Luna did I love my girl. I didn't even look back, knowing my sister was likely holding Ingr's arm to peek out around her.

Then I looked at Bex, who was shaking his head as he sheathed his weapon. "You are your mother's daughter. If I weren't looking at you just then, I would have sworn it was Laney speaking."

I gave a crooked smile as I cocked my head in apology for adding a layer of complexity to an otherwise straightforward trip. But there was nothing for it. Not only was it the right thing to do, but Shanny was counting on me and I would not let her, or her... siblings, down.

I asked him, "Can we get them safely on the Outrider or the Jewel until I can speak with the Duke?"

He nodded and smirked. Hey! That was the smirk he always gave mom! I grumped at him as he grinned and showed his empty hands to the children. "Come with me while we sort this clusterfu... ummm, mess out. And let's get you fed and into some better clothes along the way shall we? Tell me, do you like science?"

They all looked at Shan and she nodded, cupping Kes' cheek. "It's ok, Uncle Bex is one of the good ones. I'll be along shortly. My big sis can get this all sorted out in no time. She's amazing."

After a couple heartbeats of indecision, they all silently nodded and moved forward to walk with Bex. I glanced up and nudged my chin toward them. Sarafine gave me a glare, I glared right back. She hissed out a choice Gypsy curse under her breath, then seemed to blend into the shadows. I would have believed that she had just disappeared if I hadn't tasted her magic receding along with her frustrated emotions.

I knew it was killing her not to be watching over her charges, but we were surrounded by security at the moment. These kids were important to Shan, so they were important to me, and as far as a backup for Uncle Bex went, there were only three people in this world more deadly than Sara, and two of them were my moms, the third being Gramma Ranelle.

I looked at Shanny, peeking around Ingr's skirts, and narrowed an eye at her. My girl said, "Oh put that glare away." Then to my sis, she said as she pulled her in front of her and kissed the top of her head, "I won't let your big scary sister get you."

The toothy and smug grin my sis was beaming at me had me rolling my eyes. The two of them together being all defiant was too adorable. I pointed at Shan. "Spill, lady."

Then all of us girls were chuckling when Hani blurted, "Wait, where has Sora Shanicia been? I hadn't realized she was gone. Would someone care to share just what in the name of Heaven's Gate is going on here?"

CHAPTER 5 – SLIPPING OUT

The rest of the day was filled with explanations to the Duke and Duchess, flashes sent to our moms and King George while Ingr tended to the people who were ill from drinking the water from the river and well with her healing magics. Then Shanicia, Commander of the Junior Regiment met with the local chapter to share the news and developments as well as new programs for them.

It was really inspiring to me that she knew each by name, and always made eye contact when speaking with them. Making them feel and understand that what they were doing was important. I couldn't have handed the reins to a better person when I had to step down when I became a Squire.

To her credit, Duchess Aisha was incensed about the Weavers, and the way her eyes burned in a controlled rage reminded me a lot of the Harbinger of Wexbury, my mother, Lady Celeste. It was that same intensity and feeling that you were in the presence of an apex predator. While Duke Rojah was an imposing man who was no doubt a formidable and skilled combatant one wouldn't wish to cross steel with on the battlefield, it was easy to see that Aisha was the more dangerous one of the two.

She had hissed low, "These reprehensible people will be brought to justice, mark my words." And the Duke only stood at her shoulder to solemnly nod his agreement, having just a bit more restraint of his emotions. They didn't pound at my mental wall as sharply as his wife's.

And it wasn't so much the theft of palace secrets, it was that they had used children in such a manner. And if I thought the Weavers may very well pay the ultimate price for their choices before, I knew the hangman's noose was their likely fate now. Would... I mean, I know Shan was afraid of them and all, but they were sort of her parents once upon a time, would their deaths leave an emotional scar on her?

I suddenly felt my age, a teen not knowing if I had done the right thing. I've never wished harder that mom was here to take over the situation. She always knew what the right thing to do was.

By the time we ate last meal, the Weavers still hadn't been located. It was as if they knew they were being hunted and had gone to ground somewhere. We chose to eat in the lavish suites they had assigned to us. And we made all the guards stay in the corridors, only Aunt Sara was in the rooms somewhere with us as we couldn't stop her if we wished.

I went over the flashes from both Highland and Templar Hall, as well as copies of the flash conversations between our mothers and King George and Queen Everly. Mom was insistent that the children were made safe above all else, and she had stated, "As the Weavers are of the Altii, and these are your final days as Prime Ruler before you force the burden on me, I leave the matters of the crimes and probable treason to the Crown to you, George. But the children need to be with someone they know and trust right now, they were Shanny's kin, so they need to be with her while I, in my capacity Great Mother, will put them under my protection until this can all be sorted."

Everly had responded, and I could just picture her sly smirk in my head as I read it, "And here you think you're no diplomat, Laney dear. I can't imagine what the poor babies have been through, of course, Sparo will do all to assure their nightmare comes to an end."

George added, "Recall the girls before they get it into their heads that they need to handle this. All of them, including our Shavon, are too bullheaded, brash... and young, to put themselves in possible danger when Hell's Gate has some of the most skilled Knights in all of Sparo."

The response I just knew had to be from mother instead of mom, as it read, "Herding cats, George. Herding cats."

I can imagine the man's booming laughter at reading that. "There is that, Celeste."

Then there were the expected flashes from mom and the "Crown" for us to end our trip on the morrow and depart from Hell's Gate. I handed the one from Everly to Shavon, telling her it was time for her to come home too."

I smirked as she rolled her eyes at it. "They treat us like children."

A resigned voice from the rafters called out, "Because you are all children, Highness."

Desi chuckled and said to the ceiling, "Nobody asked for input, Ghost."

I bit my tongue to prevent a smile and snort. Ever since mom stuck Sara with us as our personal guard, she's always been in the shadows, watching over us. People only catch fleeting glances of her and most of Sparo has taken to calling her the Ghost of the Lupei. It rankles her tail-feathers but we enjoyed knowing that Sparo knew who she was, and the important and sometimes impossible job she was tasked to.

Then Shavon added cutely, squinting her eyes to try to locate her in the shadows, "But we love you anyway."

Ingr just nodded then looked directly at our pseudo-aunt, likely feeling her magiks too, "Love you."

"And that's why I love you two as well. The trouble twosome, not so much."

"Hey!"

"I tease, my Sora."

Shan just tossed a tangerine, which had likely been airlifted from Far Reach, up into the rafters. And I smelled the tangy citrus smell as she started peeling it. "Ok, I like the tiny impulsive one too."

I harrumphed, shooting a toothy grin at her. Then my eyes widened a bit as I remembered the little vial Amelia had slipped me. I pulled it out of a belt pouch and held it up to the electric lights that were masquerading as candles in the chandelier. It was perfectly clear.

Shan said from where she was looking over my shoulder, her cheek on mine as she squinted, "Looks like water."

I nodded then took the stopper off of it, and was transported back to the Avalon war for a second as I caught a whiff of a familiar smell that was, well, watered down from what I remember. I shuddered, I haven't had a flashback like that in a long time. I whispered, "Avalon," As Ingr steadied me, concern painting her delicate features.

I looked up, then through the east windows to the darkening sky, the debris ring around the Earth reflecting light and the Beacon of Great Mother Laney stretching far off into the stars at an oblique angle from this distance from it. Thousands of miles from the lands of the D.C. and the fallen Lady where all of mom's magics combined to create that beacon of hope to all who saw it.

"I know what the sickness is. There is that caustic fuel Avalon refines from the black tars to run their motorized vehicles, tainting the water. Amelia spoke of Purist activity to the East, along the river. They must be dumping fuel into the river. But to what end? What can they accomplish? If it was just to kill the people of Hell's Gate, there are more direct and effective ways to accomplish that. And they're killing the land too."

Shavon made a thoughtful sound and we all turned to her, she got the same embarrassed look Shan always got when she thought she was interrupting. When none of us spoke as we stared at her she sighed and said, "Maybe that's the point. Killing the land that is.

And it has the added benefit of sickening the people and animals too."

Ingr furrowed her brow. "To what end? It will take some doing and multiple healers, but I was able to stop the progression of the people afflicted with the poisoning. With a couple more healing sessions we can help them recover from its effects."

The princess nodded, face screwed up in thought. "True, but how much time would it take to gather enough healers in one place, I hear it is a rare magik even among the People. And would the Mountain Gypsies wish these rare healers all bunched up in one place? And what about the wildlife?"

She held up a stalling hand as she said, "From what we've gathered, Hell's Gate is keeping its livestock which hasn't been affected yet away from the tainted water, but what about the wildlife that relies upon the river for survival? They say they have patrols on the riverbank to gather the dead animals, birds, and fish so that the tainted bodies don't further sicken the scavengers and other wildlife."

Then she finished with, "It will take dozens of Techromancers of the nature element months to clean the contaminants from the river banks and soil. It may as well be salted earth. And this valley is virtually the only bastion of life in their realm. If they were forced to abandon it to the realms to the west... the mines of my old home here would be virtually abandoned. And they account for sixty percent of all the rare metals production in the Lower Ten."

I just blinked. Was that what was going on here? Not a bad attempt at poisoning the people here, but an attempt to make the area unlivable so that the Avalon Purists could make not a land grab, but a resource grab. It had all the earmarks of the old guard of Avalon, exploiting the resources of other lands like parasites. I was so glad that those who perpetuated that kind of thinking there have been overthrown, and more level heads, ruled Avalon fairly and respectfully.

I really liked President Cutter, and so did most of Avalon save the Purists who have her labeled as a traitor because she would rather see the people of Avalon survive and thrive rather than being run into the ground by their caustic thinking and actions which necessitated all the other known lands at the time to revolt and raise arms against them.

Then with a mental growl, I wondered if any of this had to do with the sightings of that psycho, Aelwen. If she was teaming up with the Purists now, as she has with marauders, then she was slowly assembling a base of power... which is her M.O. Was she... was she building an army?

When I looked around to see all eyes were on me, I realized I must have said some of that aloud. I felt my cheeks burning then shrugged. "There's only one way to find out for sure."

Shavon said, sounding skeptical and a little concerned, "But if Duke Rojah, or more importantly, Duchess Aisha, since she appears scarily competent and dangerous like Sora Celeste, haven't located the perpetrators yet, how can..."

Shanny chirped out, her chest puffing up in pride, "They didn't have a living life detector, Mist can feel life and emotion. If people are hiding out on the river, she can find them."

Ingr snagged her arm to pull her back to her so she could wrangle her better, adding, "And we have a piece of intelligence nobody else has. Amelia of the Aratraya gave us a possible starting point."

"How did she come by that particular..."

I just said, mimicking Grammy Rain's mysterious tone, "The Altii are yet young, and the People have ways of... sussing things out."

Standing, I grabbed my belt and checked the packs and weapons in their scabbards, then said to the group, "Ok ladies, I'll need a guide and a diversion."

I heard Sara tsking from above and just pointed up behind myself without looking to say, "Nobody asked you if this was a good idea, woman." Her chuckling came from the shadows.

Laying out my harebrained plan I prompted with an apology, "Shavon, we'll need Hani in here. He'll know how to get me outside the keep without being seen." I knew the boy would be hopeful and accept an invitation from the Crowned Princess because, well, he's a boy. I know it was shameless, but this was serious business. It didn't make sense to get the Duke involved until we confirmed our wild-ass guess.

"Ingr and Shanny, I'll need you two to divert the attention of our guards so that they don't realize I'm no longer in the suite."

My girl cocked a brow at me, oh shit, that was her, "What do you think you're doing, tala?"

I melted inside every time she called me tala. The Mountain Gypsy word has no equivalent in English. Roughly translated it means one who is held dear in one's heart. She uses it for Shanicia too, but when she says it to me, there is always a heat to it, well maybe I just feel the heat because her emotions radiated so warmly when she uttered it.

"You're not going anywhere without me."

Shan blurted, "Or me."

Ingr shot her the look one gave someone precious to you who is misbehaving, "No, this is dangerous little tala. You have to stay here where..."

I interrupted, pointing at her, "No and..." I pointed at my little sis, "No." There was no way I was bringing two of the people I most loved into danger, so I put a spin on it, "One of us sneaking out may be missed by the army of guards assigned to us, but a group of us going missing is likely to raise the alarm."

Then I challenged before they could argue, "Besides, I'm quite sure Aunt Sara isn't going to let me out of her sight, and if any trouble pops up, I dare you to say that she can't handle it."

They had almost matching annoyed but screwed up faces, lips pushed to one side as their eyes narrowed in thought as they digested that. I wonder if Ingr realizes how much of her personality Shan has adopted. When my love just made an exasperated sound, I grinned in triumph until she pointed a warning finger at me and I refrained from celebrating.

Then the Sora of the Lupei said to my little sister, "Ok, we'll have to keep any external attention on us." Then to me, "I'm not at all happy about you slipping out alone, we'll have words later."

I tried an experimental toothy grin of apology. Doh! No, go. Some Misty was in trouuuuuble. But that was later, just then I needed to... "Shavon?"

She exhaled then warned, "I'm with them on this, lady," before huffing and marching to the door. She opened it enough to stick her head out and we heard her and someone else murmuring. Then she pulled back in and said, "An invitation has been sent to Hani."

"Eeeexcelllent."

Then faster than we expected, there was a knock on the door, and Hani's voice called out, "Princess?"

Shavon gave me... the look. Then she called out sweetly, "Come in."

The boy slipped in, imposing as ever with his looming height and well-toned physique. The bundle of flowers in his hand and the hopeful look were both dashed when he saw all of us grinning at him like a pack of wolves. His hand dropped to his side as he held the flowers limply. "Ah. I may have misinterpreted things a..."

Shavon sighed, looking apologetic, but pointed out, "I'm not of courting age yet, man, get a grip."

He started to defend but saw her smirk indicating she teased the poor boy. She pointed at me and he turned, inclined his head, and I squinted one eye. "Umm... I don't suppose you ever snuck out of the palace to make mischief as you grew up?"

The grin on his face told me he had a rebellious streak in him I wouldn't have thunk. "Mischief is in my repertoire. Why do you ask, and more importantly, will it vex my parents?"

Ok, I was re-evaluating the boy now, and couldn't help but liking him. We all looked at each other and in silent agreement, I laid it all out for him. "So I need to get out of the keep unseen, and need a guide upriver to where our intel says there may be something to point us to the people doing this to your realm."

He nodded slowly, thoughtfully, and I could see the decision made as he said as he strode to the back corner of the suite. "I've been crawling around inside the Palace all my life, and I know all the secrets, like..." He pushed at a narrow tapestry and the wall, stones and all, pivoted in as he finished, "...where all the hidden servant's corridors are." He shot us all a roguish grin full of mirth and mischief.

"Brilliant!"

I gave Shan a kiss on top of her head and pecked Ingr's lips where she was pointing expectantly, then I winked at Shavon and said to them all, "We'll be back before you know it. A quick reconnoiter and back to the Palace for us."

Then Hani and I slipped into the dim corridors behind the walls, a tangy magik following us though I couldn't see how Sarafine was following in the shadows.

I nodded to myself as we made good time, this would be quick like I promised, what could possibly go wrong?

CHAPTER 6 – EVERYTHING WENT WRONG

I've learned my lesson now, not to jinx yourself like that. At first, things went well, Hani brought us through a maze of corridors, skillfully avoiding the sentries blocking the entrance to the corridors adjacent to the suites we were in. I appreciated how thorough Hani's parents were about assuring our safety and privacy.

I'm not sure the masters of all the keeps of other realms would have thought to secure the servant halls, not that they wouldn't think it was a risk, but because they would likely not have even thought of it. Most of the realms' nobles liked their servants not seen nor heard so they had these back halls to facilitate that. Out of sight, out of mind. I was glad Wexbury had very few and Templar Hall didn't incorporate them at all, and our workers get paid a modest stipend for their services.

Then after so many twists and turns, we wound up in a larder somewhere, I think it may have been adjacent to one of the palace kitchens by the scintillating aromas making their way into the space. It was there I glanced around, a sneaking suspicion niggling at the back of my mind that I knew what this was.

The young Marquess gave me a sly grin as he reached behind a wooden rack holding sacks of grain and flour that looked to be built into the stone wall, and with an almost inaudible clank, the entire rack hinged out a couple inches. He winked as he held a finger to his lips and pulled on the rack, swinging it out almost soundlessly on well-maintained hinges.

My eyes adjusted to the pitch-black tunnel beyond as my power rose in me to see down the tunnel clearly. The Hell's Gate bolthole!

Every keep and castle has a bolthole. It is a secret exit used by the Dukes and Duchesses to escape if the castle is overrun. They are closely guarded secrets. There are trained masons in every Duke's guard, who lay the foundations for any new keeps or castles. So when the other masons are brought in to construct the castle, the bolthole is already in place and none of the workers know of its existence.

Only the Duke's family and the Knights of the realm know where the bolthole is located and where it exits the castle or keep. I know where the Wexbury Bolthole is because my moms shared it with me when I became Squire, and I accidentally know where the Highland Reach bolthole is since that is how the Ex-Duchess Aelwen escaped after kidnapping me. Now I know Hell's Gate's.

Why would Hani share this with... oh... nevermind, I forget that I am supposedly royalty now so would be expected to know the locations of all the boltholes in Sparo. Once I am knighted, my moms say they will be teaching me all the secrets I should know as the heir, the mostenitor of the mantle of Great Mother of Sparo.

He started to strike a flint and steel over a torch by the entrance. I sighed and put a halting hand on his arm. "I'll guide us, just shut the door."

He heaved, pulling the rack back in place, swallowing us in darkness, and a latch made a metallic clunk. "How will you gui..."

"Magic."

"What do... oh, I'm so dense at times. Of course, you're a nature elemental, you hold a spark. Is it true Techromancers can see as clearly in the dark as they can in the light of Father Sol?"

I shook my head, and almost slapped it as I looked at the poor boy staring at the wrong spot as he spoke to me. He can't see you nodding, Mist. I took his elbow and started dragging him down the tunnel at a jog. "Not exactly, we can see clearly, but most, not all, color is washed out because of the hue of our magic. It even happens when we use our power in daylight, but sunlight is much brighter than our own spark, so it isn't very pronounced then."

He nodded. "Ah, so like when you look through stained glass, the world takes on the different hues of whichever piece you are looking through."

"Exactly. Perceptive."

"Perceptive is my nickname."

"Seriously?"

"No."

I chuckled. "I have to be honest, at first I thought you'd be a stick in the mud like most noble children, but you're ok, Hani."

Now he chuckled as we approached what looked like a dead-end, "You talk like you're exempt from that."

I slowed us to a stop at a stone wall as I regarded him. Did he truly not know? Scholars and bards have been studying and compiling information about mom... well since the battle of the Monolith. I just assumed it was common knowledge.

"You do know I was a Cobbler before my moms fostered me, don't you? And that Great Mother Laney was a Herder, and Sora Celeste, the Harbinger of Wexbury, was a Trapper?"

He cocked a brow as he reached a hand tentatively forward to touch the wall. Then as he moved to the side and felt for a torch sconce, he prompted, "All commoners, truly?"

I sighed, thinking he was looking down on the fact, but again the boy surprised me when he said as he pulled the sconce and with a clank a portion of the wall separated at a seam, "That's amazing! That should open the eyes of some of these hidebound curmudgeons of the old guard that it makes no difference your station in life, all are capable of greatness, noble or not."

I gave him a crooked smile and we slipped out into the night. I looked back to see we were not just out of the palace, but the keep as well. This was some sort of back alley by the Bazaar. He pulled the stone slab back in place, hearing the locking mechanism engage, then he pushed his shoulder with great effort against it to verify it was secure.

I told him, "Very forward-thinking. You're just full of surprises, aren't you?"

He just grinned at the compliment, then shared, "When my parents told me they wanted me to enter into a courtship with you, I was frustrated and upset that I had no say in my own pairings, and was relieved that you were already in a relationship. But now I find myself a little disappointed since you aren't the snooty royal I had envisioned you to be."

"Gee thanks."

"Why do women always..."

"Losing points Marquess."

"Zipping it. Well after you tell me where we are trying to get to."

He opened a small beat-up storage bench and pulled out a couple ragged cloaks, wrapping himself in one and wrapping a scrap of cloth around and around his head, making some sort of intricate head covering an effective disguise.

Then he held another cloak out to me and I rolled my eyes and pulled my hood up on my cloak, and I could see myself starting to blur. With the weight of the magiks on the cloak and the copious number of luck runes invisibly etched in it, nobody would get a good look at me or my face even if they were looking directly at me.

"Fair enough. How do I get a cloak like that?"

I smirked and said coyly, "Get adopted into a Gypsy family. I'm part of the Lupei, and they take care of their own. They don't usually let the Altii possess their magik unless it is benign charms like keeping water in a waterskin cool and sweet. But mom is half Mountain Gypsy, and, well, I'm her daughter."

He seemed to contemplate that as he squinted to try to see my face better. "But as a blended society now, shouldn't they be more forthcoming with those magiks if they are as versatile as the whispers on the wind say."

I cocked a brow. "When Hell's Gate decides to just freely give the metals of your mines to those who can use them, and the other Altii realms do the same in the way of the People, then maybe they will. But as you can see, there must be parity for all of this to work. So the more the Altii open up to the People, the more the People will reciprocate."

To his credit, his brow furrowed as he seemed to contemplate my words. "I guess we've just seen it as the People not fully embracing the new dual culture, but perhaps we should look in the mirror before we cast stones."

Snorting I teased, "How many metaphors can you butcher in the experience of one thought, Han?"

He grinned hugely, his stark white teeth a contrast to his ebony complexion. He shoved my shoulder in jest as we started down the alley. Then he froze and took a knee. "Sorry, Highness. I didn't mean to be so familiar, I should never have laid hands on you."

Mother Luna just kill me now. I sighed in exasperation as I strode past him. "You're not going to be a very good guide from down there. And drop the Highness shit, it's Misty."

He jumped up and hustled to my side as I shared again what Amelia said. He nodded and then just started walking quickly through the Bazaar, which to my surprise still had many people moving about. Sure it was a fraction of the number during the day, but still a decent number. The Wexbury and Templarville markets closed at dark. The space was lit by flickering oil lamps in the central area, but flickering electric lights on the buildings. It was a neat effect that made it look like flickering flames to match the lamps.

I noted Amelia was just tucking the last of her stock into the rolling table and lifting one end by the handles to start leaving. Her sharp eyes caught us moving through, I think she recognized the blurring effect around me as Gypsy magik, because she inclined her head our way, and smiled in satisfaction.

It appeared she knew what we were up to and she approved that I was acting on the information she had supplied. I just pulled my hood back long enough to reveal myself to her as I inclined my head back.

Then her eyes swung above us and widened a bit. I had to grin to myself, I could feel Aunt Sara's magic on the rooftops. How she had known where we would exit the keep is a question I didn't wish to ask. Mother Udele and Great Mother Ranelle always made their way into Wexbury Keep after the portcullis gates lowered for the night. Mom has always had a sneaking suspicion that they were using the Wexbury bolthole. With how skilled the People were with acquiring information, she says she wouldn't be surprised if they knew every bolthole better than the Dukes themselves.

Once we got clear of the most heavily populated area of town,

Hani led me to the riverbank. I noted that there were no buildings on either bank within around a hundred yards. They kept it as a natural area, that seemed filled with wildlife to my senses. Sick wildlife, just like the vegetation on the bank as it seemed to be spreading inland as the soil took on the contaminate.

And we made good time without having to dodge people and buildings. I prompted in a whisper. "Has it made it to the food crops yet?"

He nodded his head. "The sickness is encroaching on them and has already fouled the rice paddies."

I crouched at the bank and he followed suit. Placing a hand on the oily feeling sand, I slowly bunched my fist as I let some magic flow to reach out to the sick land. Seconds later, the toxin puddled below my hand, and an area a dozen yards around seemed to wake up and the brown of dead or dying vegetation was overwhelmed by fresh green growth.

I gasped and he steadied me, doing precision work was rough for me. I was more of an explosive results sort of magic user, like Gramma Rain, and the more control I needed the more strain it put on my body and mind, except for when I commune with animals since that is barely a trickle of magic at all.

Pointing at the puddled toxin I shared, "The Crown will send nature elementals to help heal the land like this and pull this poison from the land."

He was just blinking as he whispered excitedly, "That... was...

amazing! Dad is an elemental but since I am not, he never shares what his magic can do like this." Then he asked, "Why does my realm have so few who ever ignite?"

I shrugged. "Nobody really knows, but the People believe it has to do with proximity with Father Stone. And I tend to think they may be on to something. I've spent hours listening to the voices on the wind in the Whispering Walls, and after a while, they start to resonate with my magic, and I swear I heard my own voice in those maddening whispers."

The memory made me shudder involuntarily since I swear that I heard myself but with a much more mature voice, teasing me... then Ingr's laugh as she was saying it was bedtime and our daughter wanted me to tuck her in. I mean, how can that be? Was it a glimpse into what might come? Was it how mom experienced her seeings of probable futures?

He was just staring at me, eyes wide like he was listening to a story at the campfire.

Shaking my head to clear it, I stood and made an ushering motion. When we had traveled about the distance indicated by Amelia, I felt many points of life to the left of the riverbank. I held a hand up to stop Hani from continuing, then I whispered, "There are people nearby, lots of them. I notice there aren't many dwellings or buildings around here."

"This is by the fish farms and agricultural areas, only a few farmhouses in the area."

I nodded, knowing that was why whatever was going on was in this area. "Thank you. You need to get back to the keep, this is dangerous just to be here if it is Purists, they may have Avalon gun weapons and I don't need to get you hurt or worse."

He sighed heavily and drew his blade, a look of determination on his face. I sighed, drew Anadelea, and then started creeping forward until we could hear voices. That's when everything went wrong.

CHAPTER 7 – AELWEN

My blood chilled when I heard voices in Outsider. Damn it, marauders.

Then a man speaking with an Avalonian accent blurted out, "English ya damn savage. Where is she? She's late. She was supposed to bring us information and supplies to help us chase these other savages off the land in this god-forsaken furnace of an Outland. And the bitch promised some magic users for protection."

"If you disparage the Duchess again, I'll wear your tongue on my necklace. She's a very careful woman. She didn't assemble an army by being reckless. She'll be here."

Shitty shit shit. They truly were working with Aelwen.

Then I heard an arrow loose in a tree just behind the figures talking. We'd been spotted! I was starting to spin away to dodge the shot and slap the shaft away with the flat of my blade when a small shadow stepped in front of me with a tiny blade. With a little ping, the tip of Shanicia's dagger struck the tip of the incoming arrow, deflecting it harmlessly into the air as she looked back at me with a toothy grin, "Hi?"

I blurted, "Shanny! What are you doing here!"

And that's when the shouting began. Marauders and... by the Three Sisters! Magic users by the feel of it... rogues! All charged at us from the shadows all around the clearing, drawing weapons and spooling their magics.

I almost panicked when Ingr's hand rested on my shoulder as she started spooling her own magik, and my heart hammered in my chest as Shavon stepped behind Shanicia with her extremely thin blade drawn. What the hells? Could nobody listen?

A tangy magic flared as Aunt Sara stepped in front of us all, blade drawn and her power building fast. There was nothing for it then, I called out, "Girls, behind me!" as Hani and I stepped to either side of Sarafine, and we engaged. Steel striking steel, Sara somehow grounding out all the magics thrown our way while Hani and I danced around my aunt, intercepting all who tried to get to her as she dealt with the magical assault.

To my eternal shame, it felt like an exciting, macabre dance to me as I advanced, blocking parrying, and counterstriking. It was almost too easy when I used an upsweep reverse hand block with my dagger to keep my first opponent's arm overextended as Anadelea slashed across his belly, meeting no resistance as he wore no armor.

Was I morally soiled to have no remorse as I took a life? Did I have the right to end the spark of another human life like that? There wasn't time to contemplate as other marauders roared their defiance and charged to try to overwhelm me.

Three fell screaming as cuts and wounds opened all over them as Ingr let loose with her healing magics, only instead of healing, it did the opposite, and reopened every wound and injury the men had had in their entire lives all at once.

Hani was a beast as he engaged two big brutes who were swinging a war hammer and some sort of bone blade at the same time. They were about the same size and bulk of muscle as him, but he had a speed they couldn't match as his curved scimitar-looking blade made quick work of them in that figure eight attack many Hell's Gate knights used.

Shavon and Shan seemed to be in tune with each other, Shan going low as her sister went high, deflecting blows after sweeping blow from a gangly man with filed teeth. While I took on two club-wielding men, I threw my Templar dagger sideways and the man went down with a gurgling scream as the knife sank into his throat.

I heard a swish above my head the wind of the passing blade rustling my hood and one of my opponents fell to Sara's sweeping blade. I scanned the engagement, two dozen more men were coming at us, and the Avalonians seemed too shocked to engage yet. I saw the smoking bodies of three men in the middle of it all and realized I couldn't feel the rogues' magics anymore.

I hesitated when I saw behind them all, the Weavers! They were looking nervous and appeared to be seconds from bolting.

When the man in front of me telegraphed a blow, I stepped into him as I ducked the sweeping strike instead of retreating, then I hooked his overextended arm and rolled across his back as I dipped to hook a leg. I screamed with the effort of the move that mother made look so easy as I stood tall, stretching the man's back across my shoulders, then I dropped to a knee as I yanked down. With a sickening crack, the man's back snapped and I just released him, letting his body fall back to the ground.

Hani was looking at me in shock, muttering, "The Harbinger's Hammer!"

Then familiar amused laughter came from the shadows as a voice that grated on me and my memories called out, "That's enough boys." And as the girls, Sara, and Hani all formed up around me, the rogue Duchess Aelwen stepped from the shadows, her otherwise beautiful features marred by the crooked and lumpy nose that had been broken multiple times... by me and Shan, and healed improperly. The marauders disengaged and formed up around the woman as she just strode forward.

"Misty, darling. I just wanted to see if you've lost your touch. They weren't really going to do you harm. How long has it been since New Cali?" Then she spun at the sound of an Avalon gun weapon chambering a round. And one of the five men with purple armbands swung the weapon my way.

I pulled at the life under his feet, intending on ending the man with a dozen saplings before he had the chance to fire on me, but Aelwen screeched out in incensed fury, "No!" And her magic, which she always suppressed and kept hidden from everyone, slammed into the man. With no place for the raw, unformed energy to go to the ground, the man screamed as his skin boiled and flesh was burned off his arm. He was flung back and his lifeless body was caught by his countrymen.

She strode toward the Avalonians pointing back at me. "Nobody messes with the Gypsy bitch or her kin here but me! I told you that when I arranged this meeting tonight. If we take the brats... no offense Misty, sweetie, and little Shanny... then we'd have the co-ruler of all of Sparo in our pockets and we wouldn't need to continue your ludicrous plan of poisoning the land as you did in the Outlands. We'd have all the resources we need here. You'd have gotten your revenge on Sparo."

Shan was actually growling when she realized the Weavers were there and part of this whole mess, her eyes were glowing slightly in her anger the tiny spark of a sensitive exerting itself.

I noted all the barrels behind the Avalonians, by a group of those two-wheeled motorized vehicles Avalon scouts and assassins preferred. I knew the barrels had to contain that caustic byproduct from making their fuel.

The leader of the Purists almost spat as he sputtered out, "You killed him! And it's your delusions that the Kingdom Killer would ever bend to your demands that have exposed us! We were crazy to have agreed to work with a psychotic bitch like you."

She cocked a brow and said, "Oh really now. Fine, partnership terminated." She swirled a finger in the air and on cue, a huge lumbering shape rose from behind the rise behind her, deep whupping sounds now apparent coming from the only surviving Avalonian gunship. And where the long gun nests had been which shot multiple metal projectiles per second, that mom had disabled, were men behind some sort of huge hand-cranked crossbows on the platforms on either side of the gondola.

They started cranking and hell rained down! My eyes widened as the contraptions were somehow rapid-firing huge arrows, igniting their tips as they fired, and blinding light had us covering our eyes as the burning magnesium arrowheads lit up the world brighter than Father Sol as the projectiles peppered the two-wheeled, black smoke belching transports, and the barrels. Had they modeled them after the Hell's Gate airship armaments?

I don't know if it was the magnesium burning through their fuel tanks or igniting the barrels, but a series of explosions rocked the ground. The Avalonians dove to the ground, covering their heads. Then it was all silent as one of the repeating crossbows trained on the Avalonians and one on us.

That stayed Sara's hand as I had felt her tense as she started spooling her own magics again, much weaker now, to throw at the rogue Duchess.

She told the Purists, "Now run fast and far if the Burning Desert doesn't kill you, Duke Rojah will sic his dog, Duchess Aisha, on you and she will hunt you down for bringing harm to their little oasis here."

The leader started to make a threat but was silenced when, in a bright flare, two arrows struck at his feet, the burning magnesium hissing and smoking. Then he hissed as he backed off with the others, "This isn't over, snake. We'll come for you once Avalon is free of Sparo occupation."

She yawned and waved him off airily, the scar on her hand apparent from where mom had flung an iron penny through it. Then she said as if contemplating out loud as I prepared to take down the airship the moment it dipped low enough for me to send trees shooting up from the ground to foul the propellers and puncture the lift envelope. I'd have to be careful, the Avalon airship used hydrogen, not helium and any spark could ignite the whole thing. I really wished mom was here, she'd know how best to protect the others.

That's when I noted the Weavers were no longer in the clearing. The snakes took the opportunity of the explosions to slither off again. And I noted Shan was scanning the darkness for them too.

The rogue duchess shared, "Imagine my surprise and delight when my spies in the Hell's Gate home battalion told me that you and your sister would be visiting Hell's Gate, Misty, dear. Then the pot got even sweeter when the Crowned Princess herself decided to come. In one fell sweep, I can have both leaders of Sparo under my thumb."

She absently nudged one of the dead magic users with her toe and hmmed before looking up at Sarafine, "You broke my rogues, now I'll have to recruit more. They're getting harder to come by now that commoners using magic is no longer illegal." Then she tutted, raising a finger. "Uh uh uh, I wouldn't't." She pointed at the airship and the stock of the second repeating crossbow swung our way.

Aunt Sara's hand dropped from where she had been moving it ever so slowly to one of her throwing knives.

I muttered, "You're still a psycho, Aelwen. Let the others go and let's finish this, you and me."

She blinked at me then tilted her head back and laughed, tittering out, "You are your mother's daughter. What in our past dealings would make you believe I'm a fool, little Gypsy child? I saw what you did in Avalon. You're likely more dangerous than Ranelle herself. Why would I give up these pawns when their safety is the only thing stopping you from ending me right now?"

Then her smile dropped. "Really, Misty, I still don't know why you're still cross with me, it was only business. I'm rather quite fond of you..." She rubbed her poorly healed nose absently. "Even though your greetings could use some work. I am your favorite auntie am I not?" The woman was deranged and I absently wondered if she believed her own words.

She reached to her hip and tossed two sets of Faraday cage cuffs to the ground in front of Sara and me. "Shall we retire to the airship ladies?" Then she called out loudly toward the dirigible as it hovered there, giant propellers whupping the air, "I don't need the boy, you can..." My eyes widened and all of us stepped in front of Hani. The bitch was going to execute him!

And that's when we heard it, it started as a thrumming and vibration in the ground. Then we could hear men shouting as horses' hooves pounded the Earth approaching rapidly. There must have been an entire regiment approaching! A knight of Hell's Gate burst out into the clearing and shouted back, "They're here!"

Aelwen growled out an exasperated sound and then said as she made a motion with her hand, "That would be my cue to exit. Damn interfering knights! I'd ask for a goodbye hug from you and little Shanicia for your favorite auntie, but I quite like my nose not broken girls. Give my love to your mother, will you?"

The end of a rope ladder landed at her feet and she stepped onto it as the airship started to peel off and gain altitude quickly. One of the crossbows was still trained on us and the other started spitting brightly flaring projectiles at the approaching knights. For a split second, I was torn. I could stop Aelwen, tangle her ladder up in branches, or I could...

I made my own exasperated sound as I spun toward the knights, thrusting my hand forward, screaming in frustration and strain while the ground in front of them exploded as I willed the roots to grow into a solid barrier of tree trunks as I accelerated their aging instantly. The burning magnesium arrows all struck and ignited the wall that shielded the knights.

Then I spun back to see the airship was already beyond my reach and leaving even the range of any archers. Aelwen actually blew us a little kiss as the vessel turned toward the Uninhabitable Lands and the Eastlands where we believed she has taken refuge. A land that does not allow Sparo to visit.

Shanny squeaked out, "I hate that psycho bitch."

Ingr reprimanded, "Language, tala."

Shan looked sheepish and we all winced when Sara swore, "Rahat!"

That's when dozens of knights and our security detachment, led by Duke Rojah and Duchess Aisha themselves wheeled around the burning wall of trunks between us, dozens of arrows loosing toward the retreating airship and falling short, while others circled the remaining marauders that Aelwen just abandoned.

I noted with wry amusement how they had likely found us out here, as Amelia was off to the side on a small mustang, the horses the People preferred. She inclined her head slightly to me, a wry grin on her face.

The Duke looked down at us from on top of his midnight black steed, then the surrendering marauders and bodies around the clearing before glancing one last time at Aelwen's retreat, all while Aisha had slid off her horse and was checking her son frantically for injury.

Then the big man slid off his horse, laugh booming as he inclined his head to us. "The Great Mother sent us a flash, telling us to watch you closely because you are headstrong and likely wouldn't let the situation sit while the Crown marshaled an investigation. She worried you'd get into trouble."

He motioned toward the bodies. "Apparently, she discounted your abilities."

Then before anyone could say anything he swung his head to his son. "And you! You had your mother worried out of her mind. How could you do something so foolish?"

I had to hide a smile as the young Marquess whined as he patty-caked his mother's hands away from him, "Daaad. Please. Not in front of the princesses."

And everyone chuckled as the adrenaline burned off, leaving me shaking and holding my little sis to me.

Shavon said in a no-nonsense tone, "Right then. This was enough adventure for tonight, would anyone object to retiring back to the palace before the lectures begin?"

Duchess Aisha took us all in one at a time as she promised, "By all means, Highness... and there will be lectures... oh will there be lectures."

EPILOGUE

I looked at the construction workers in our apartment suite in Templar Hall as they shored up the ceiling where a stone wall had been removed to add rooms to the suite. Mom was beside herself with excitement.

She had taken time from all the paperwork that King George has been funneling to her in the final days before she became Prime and she would return the favor in spades. She actually rubs her hands together in anticipation of making the silly man pay for heaping all the monotonous work of running Sparo on her with a grin on his face.

Of course we couldn't get home without incident. First, Hani had spoken with Shan before we left, inquiring if he could call on her when she reached courting age. We all snickered at her, "Boys? Ewww!" My sis hasn't discovered boys yet. We had given the poor boy apologetic looks as we boarded the Jewel for the return trip.

Shanny was afraid that the other Street Rats would be separated by the Crown. And she had somehow convinced us to defy our moms and fly to Junior Regiment Headquarters down in... I still refuse to call it Shantopia. And that's where we sent a flash to them from. And just why was Aunt Sara so amused when we did it?

Our parents must have broken all flight speed records for a courier vessel getting down to us. And Shan stood tall, my traitorous girl standing behind her, hands on her shoulders for support. And I could feel the complex emotions of our moms before they stepped into the room. Mother was worried and flustered, but for some reason, amused as well.

Mom however was mad, feeling guilty, worried out of her mind, and anxious. And there was that internal battle with her own magics she was always fighting that shadowed her other feelings. I had whispered to everyone as Hak, Rual, and Kes hid behind me, peeking around my sides, "This is not going to end well."

But what happened stunned us all. Mom came stalking around the corner, in all her five-foot-nothing glory. But she filled the place with her presence as she has always done, commanding the room like a force of nature. Something she had always possessed even though she can't seem to see it. People always took notice whenever Laney of Wexbury was there. It was her need to strive to always do what was right, and having the wherewithal to actually do it, and the power to back it all up.

She had her stern, Mom face on but her eyes widened, looking almost doe-like. And I felt the nausea that hit me when she time split. Standing directly in front of me before she even moved, ghostly afterimages of herself streaking to catch up.

Her smile almost split her face as she said in wonder, "Hello," to the stunned children behind me.

I rolled my eyes, knowing the look, and smirked, realizing I was shielding my future siblings.

Mother was chuckling. "Oh, for fuck's sake," telling me she

knew the look too.

But that was nothing compared to the reaction all of our various grandparents had. None of them can stop doting on their new grandchildren, especially Grammy Margret.

And here we were, three weeks later, after the fostering of my two new brothers and another little sister was complete. And I have to tell you, they were a hoot. They all had the sly humor of Shanny, and I swear Kes was emulating her. But we were all going to have our hands full getting them out of the habit of lifting valuables from everyone they met. It's as if they can't comprehend that their new parents don't want them to steal for them. It's all they knew and my heart broke for them, and then broke all over again for Shan, realizing that was likely how she had felt too. And old habits are hard to break.

Kes dashed in squealing, Shan and the boys hot on her heels. She came running up to mom and Ingr, hiding behind them with a toothy grin on her face. The other Street Rats looked far too innocent. Then with a cute little hop, Kes left her hiding spot to land in front of me, her brown eyes glittering as she held a hand up to my shoulder.

I sighed while mom demanded, "What's going on, children? No roughhousing inside. The builders don't need the distraction." With a tiny push of magic, I had Itsy and Bitsy crawl out on my shoulder and gave them the impression of going to Kes. They scurried onto her hands and she tittered in glee as she looked at the small beasties.

It was the same wonder Shanicia had displayed when she learned I could do this.

Shan said with all the authority she could muster, "Nothing, mom. We're going to go to the market to hand out some penny vouchers. It's First Day after all."

"Ok, but be careful. And be home for last meal." Then she went about hugging and kissing them all. And the most powerful and deadly person Sparo has ever known, hugged her arms to herself when they all chimed out together, "Love you too mom." Causing mom to squish her head to her shoulders with a happy smile. Is someone so dangerous allowed to be so cute?

I watched them go, then looked to my girl, then my moms with hope as I sighed.

Mother chuckled. "Grounded means grounded, Mist. You knew what you were doing in Hell's Gate was reckless, so you're confined to the Hall for a month."

"But I'm a Squire and almost an adult."

"Be that as it may, you're also a grounded Squire."

Then Ingr asked, "May I accompany her to the market to keep track of the scamps?"

I gawked when my moms said in unison, "Of course, Ingr."

And mom added, "You were the only one with any sense on that trip."

I grumped, "Hey, why are you breaking your own rules for her and not me, your own daughter? I feel slighted."

Mom nodded, biting her tongue in amusement. "Grounded and slighted. Ingr is about to become our daughter too, and she's adorable."

Ingr nodded, acting innocent, saying in the tongue of the People, "It's true, tala." Then she shot me a nose crinkle that made me go weak in the knees, a silly smile on my face.

Everyone had a good chuckle at me, then my girl took my hand and dragged me with her, chasing down the pack of trouble.

I sighed when Mother said, "Sara?"

Reaching out with my magics I called back, "Already shadowing trouble."

And all was right in Sparo as I contemplated where our next adventure would take us.

the end

Novels by Erik Schubach

Books in the Worldship Files series...
Leviathan
Firewyrm
Cityships
Morrigan
Changeling (2021)

Books in the Techromancy Scrolls series...
Adept
Soras
Masquerade
Westlands
Avalon
New Cali
Colossus

Books in the Sparo Rising series...
Blade of Wexbury
Mason of York (coming soon)
Hammers of Flatlash (coming soon)

Books in the Urban Fairytales series...
Red Hood: The Hunt
Snow: The White Crow
Ella: Cinders and Ash
Rose: Briar's Thorn
Let Down Your Hair
Hair of Gold: Just Right
The Hood of Locksley
Beauty In the Beast
No Place Like Home
Shadow Of The Hook
Armageddon

Books in the New Sentinels series...
Djinn: Cursed
Raven Maid: Out of the Darkness
Fate: No Strings Attached

Open Seas: Just Add Water
Ghost-ish: Lazarus
Anubis: Death's Mistress
Sentinels: Reckoning (2021)

Books in the April series...
Facets of April
Shadows of April (2021)

Books in the Drakon series...
Awakening
Dragonfall

Books in the Valkyrie Chronicles series...
Return of the Asgard
Bloodlines
Folkvangr
Seventy Two Hours
Titans

Books in the Tales From Olympus series...
Gods Reunited
Alfheim
Odyssey

Books in the Bridge series...
Trolls
Traitor
Unbroken
Krynn

Books in the Fracture series...
Divergence

Novellas by Erik Schubach

The Hollow

Novellas in the Paranormals series...
Fleas
This Sucks
Jinx (2021)

Novellas in the Fixit Adventures...
Fixit
Glitch
Vashon
Descent
Sedition

Novellas in the Emily Monroe Is Not The Chosen One series...
Night Shift
Unchosen
Rechosen

Novellas in the Shadow of the Scrolls series...
Hell's Gate

Short Stories by Erik Schubach

(These short stories span many different genres)

A Little Favor
Lost in the Woods
MUB
Mirror Mirror On The Wall
Oops!
Rift Jumpers: Faster Than Light
Scythe
Snack Run
Something Pretty

Romance Novels by Erik Schubach

Books in the Music of the Soul universe...
(All books are standalone and can be read in any order)
Music of the Soul
A Deafening Whisper
Dating Game
Karaoke Queen
Silent Bob
Five Feet or Less
Broken Song
Syncopated Rhythm
Progeny
Girl Next Door
Lightning Strikes Twice
June
Dead Shot

Music of the Soul Shorts...
(All short stories are standalone and can be read in any order)
Misadventures of Victoria Davenport: Operation Matchmaker
Wallflower
Accidental Date
Holiday Morsels
What Happened In Vegas?

Books in the London Harmony series...
(All books are standalone and can be read in any order)
Water Gypsy
Feel the Beat
Roctoberfest
Small Fry
Doghouse
Minuette
Squid Hugs
The Pike
Flotilla

Books in the Pike series...
(All books are standalone and can be read in any order)
Ships In The Night

Right To Remain Silent
Evermore
New Beginnings

Books in the Flotilla series...
(All books are standalone and can be read in any order)
Making Waves
Keeping Time
The Temp
Paying the Toll

Books in the Unleashed series...
Case of the Collie Flour
Case of the Hot Dog
Case of the Gold Retriever
Case of the Great Danish
Case of the Yorkshire Pudding
Case of the Poodle Doodle
Case of the Hound About Town
Case of the Shepherd's Pie
Case of the Bull Doggish
Case of the Dalmatian Salvation
Case of the Irish Sitter

Chapter 1 – Portcullis

I yawned as I stepped out of my family's stone cottage with my little brother, Jace, the steel pin hinges groaned in protest. I closed the old wooden door as quietly as I could as to not waken mother. Her health had been deteriorating and we didn't like her exerting herself.

We walked to the pig pen and I grabbed my wooden cart by the handles and started toward the portcullis of the defensive wall around our village. I called back, "After you feed the hogs, bring Matilda to the butcher. She isn't laying anymore, and we could probably get at least two pennies for her or trade for a half sack of grain, she has some good meat on her."

He nodded as he grabbed the bucket to get some of the castoffs from Castle Wexbury we had traded some eggs for. Our feathered ladies were some of the best laying hens in the village and the lords of the castle were partial to them. I smiled. He was only seven but was a godsend around here. With mother down, he was all I had to help me with all the chores while I was out scavenging.

I was not about to marry myself off just to maintain the household, I don't care if I was of age of consent last month or not. No man would have me, ever, and I don't understand why any woman would ever betroth herself to one. I shivered at the thought.

I looked back at the door then added, "Remind me when I get back to grease the door hinges with lard or bacon grease would you? I don't want that noisy door waking mother, she needs her rest." He nodded in earnest. I smiled at him, he was such a good boy, I was proud to have him as a brother.

I started wheeling my cart to the cobbled road in the twilight of the morning. He called back, "Do you think you'll get enough today Laney?"

I smiled more confidently than I felt and crossed my fingers at him, "Let's hope this batch will get us enough for the medicines." He crossed his small fingers too and smiled and went back to the morning chores.

I walked down the lane, the village was waking up. I started passing people getting to their jobs and had to move for a couple chargers trotting gallantly past as the morning patrol went to replace the night patrol outside the walls.

I looked at them with awe and amazement. To be a noble would be so glamorous. They protect the village and we tithe them so that they can concentrate on that defense. I blinked. One had the crest with a lightning bolt crossed with a sword on her sash. A Techno Knight! I noticed my jaw was hanging open as she passed by and snapped my mouth shut. She noticed my admiration and she winked at me as she trotted past. She looked a year or two older than my nineteen years.

I blushed, she was not only a knight, but a Techno Knight. Her red hair flowed back over her armored shoulders like a cape draping over the studded leather and metal. Her emerald eyes were sharp, and they glowed with the magic potential of a Techno Knight... they seemed to swallow me whole. I looked down in embarrassment when the other knight said loudly, "Looks like you have an admirer

Celeste."

She hissed at him, "Don't be such an ass Bowyn." I kept my eyes down but I could feel her eyes on me. I had a little affinity for magic and could tell when it was focused my way. Her eyes were overflowing with it.

She kicked her horse and gave it some rein and shouted, "Hyah!" And galloped off toward the gates. I looked up to watch the other knight urge his horse to catch up. I grinned, being a mere Knight of the Realm, he was subordinate to that Techno Knight. What did he call her? Celeste? He was subordinate to Lady Celeste.

I noted the street lamps in the row I was passing were flickering. I looked at the electric filaments in the globes and they were intact. I stepped over and kicked the ceramic containment vessel which held the magic potential that powered the little copper wound generator. With a scree that was just beyond all but the hearing of the young, the bulbs brightened and remained steady. I grinned.

I absently wondered how the wizards of the old realm of the Before Times powered their tech. I have heard so many ludicrous theories. Like chemical reactions. The old buffoon who proposed it called it batteries or some other nonsense. That would be terribly inefficient, and what would you do with these... batteries... once the chemical reaction was exhausted? Throw them out and build new ones? Non renewable resources were in such short supply and that would be a waste.

But that wasn't as funny as the Techromancer who was laughed out of the conclave for suggesting that his interpretation of the old writings of the Before was that it was with water from rivers. How can water power electricity? The two do not mix. I chuckled at the thought.

No, the wizards of the Before were so much more powerful than us. Just look at all they had accomplished. We unearth more every day. They had to be so far beyond our abilities. It was only the Great Impact that brought down their civilization. I imagined all the wonders I would have seen if I had lived in their time.

As I approached the huge gates at the portcullis, I glanced back to the east, to Castle Wexbury. The great castle with it's soaring towers and waving standards. It was so large it formed two thirds of the east wall of the village itself. Well over a half mile of stone.

There, hanging above it in the sky, were the Three Sisters. The three pale white moons and the ring of debris around Earth. I tried to imagine what it would be like to see one huge moon in the sky in ancient times, before the Great Impact. A rogue astral body had collided with Mother Luna and tore her in half. I looked at her oblong egg shape and the two smaller sisters, Athena and Freya, which formed afterwards.

They say that Mother Luna will again be round one day as gravity reshapes her as she spins. She appears to be always looking down on Earth with her red eye. The pale red glow of the vast magma fields on her broken edge will eventually be swallowed. Much like the vast magma fields on the Dark Side of the Earth.

It is rumored there were billions of people in the Before. Over three quarters of the population was wiped out when the debris storm and shock wave had hit the Dark Side. And even more died in the early years. There were rumored to be huge bodies of water they called oceans that covered most of the surface of the planet. I would not have believed it if I had not seen some of the old writings that they have in the castle. The Techromancy Scrolls.

There was a picture in one, of the Earth as a blue ball, covered in water. The language looked so much like English, and I could read most of it, but the old English from the Before was so different than now. Now all villages were built by the few lakes and small rivers that came down off the Whispering Walls Mountain range in the center of the habitable lands.

The young chamber maid, Resme, who cleaned the library had been punished for letting me in to see the forbidden writings. I still feel bad for putting her in disfavor with the lords of the keep. They traded her off to another realm. She had been my only friend here.

I had to take ten lashes at the whipping post for my part. The punishment for trespass into the library was usually twenty, but the magistrate did not wish to be so harsh on a thirteen year old child. I believe he did not strike me with the enthusiasm I have seen in the past, the blows barely left any scars. He explained why the nobles were so strict with public floggings in regard to the library. The scrolls and tomes there are invaluable, and the kingdoms greatest treasure. I did not cry out, I was strong like mother told me to be.

The library had tens of thousands of scrolls and tomes that were falling apart with age. They have had Techromancers working diligently over the centuries to restore them or make modern records and reproductions so that the knowledge would not be lost to the ages.

I was knocked out of my musings when the first rays of sunlight from Father Sol crested the majestic peaks of the Whispering Walls far in the distance. I took a deep breath and looked at the line of people that was starting to form on either side of the gate. We all stayed clear of the knights, and the gate and wall guards.

A man was walking down the line with a checklist asking each person their business outside the gates. The grumpy, heavyset man wearing old, ill fitting, worn leather armor that had suffered most likely decades of disrepair, finally got to me. "Name, station, reason for travel?"

I glanced over to see the Knights just twenty feet away. I smiled a little when I saw Lady Celeste speaking with two other knights of the realm. I looked away and said to the man, "Laney Herder, serf, scavenging." We used our profession to identify ourselves, in case there were more than one person in the village with the same name. My family are livestock herders, so I had to identify myself that way.

He placed his pen down on his tablet and cuffed my ear roughly. "What are you doing scavenging you worthless tramp?! Get back to your animals, the kingdom needs food more than junk!"

I held the side of my face, my cheek stung, but I did not cry out. I worked my jaw trying to get the ringing in my ear to fade. I looked at his feet. "Please sir. I'm scavenging copper, and iron. I'm a sensitive." I pulled my crystal necklace from under my shirt, it hung on a small leather strap, it started glowing faintly amber when my hand came in contact with it.

I heard a large horse approach. A familiar woman's voice snapped out with authority, "Steward! The realm needs metals and machines from the Before as much as food! Maybe more."

He stood at sloppy attention and I kept my eyes down as he ground out, "Yes Lady Celeste. She didn't specify that at first."

Then she spoke again, "You, young miss. Are you of majority? Has your age of consent come?"

I bowed my head a little, looking at my feet. "Yes Lady."

She spoke again with a tinge of amusement in her voice, "Look up, I do not bite." I looked nervously up and she asked, "You have others to tend your animals while you are outside the gates?"

I nodded and my voice wavered when I replied, "Yes Lady. My brother. He's small but is a good worker." She smiled a little and I looked back down.

Then she asked, "You say you are a sensitive, but you said copper AND iron. Which is it?"

I chanced another look at her up on that grand mount of hers, its coat dark as midnight. "Both, Lady." I tried not to show the pride on my face. It was extremely uncommon to have the magic affinity to more than one metal. That is why I did so well on my last two outings once I was the age of majority and could travel outside the walls without an adult. I also hid the other abilities that I had started developing the past two months.

The Techromancers needed the various metals and machines to maintain and build upon the growing technology base of our village. We were one of the most advanced villages in all the realms. There was so much old technology buried just below the surface, which was so much easier and quicker to use than the mining and smelting of ore from the mines. I was able to save up fifteen iron pennies and two gold coins from my previous outings. Just one more gold coin and I could afford the medicines for mother from the hospital.

She cocked an eyebrow and gave me a genuinely surprised smile. "Truly?" I nodded and then she looked at the man. "Steward, allow this woman to the front of the line, her work is valuable to the realm."

He shot me a glare but bowed slightly to her and responded, "Lady." Then he grabbed the handles of my cart and pushed it roughly to the front of the line, cussing the whole way.

I looked up to the knight and did a curtsy and said quickly, "Thank you Lady."

She shook her head and said, "Celeste. You may call me Celeste, Laney."

I nodded and ran off to my cart. I was blushing profusely. I wondered where all my confidence had gone. I'd never felt so self conscious around anyone. Because Laney you fool, she was a Techno Knight! A Knight of the Realm! I caught myself smiling. I had just spoken to a Techno Knight, Jace was going to be so jealous!

The clock in the church steeple in the center of the village turned over to seven o'clock and the huge church bell started chiming the start of the day. The deep resonating bongs filling the valley. Lady Celeste had her horse sidle up to the receiver beside the huge motors that operated the gate. Then she drew her long sword.

The light of the rising sun reflected off of it. I could feel her magics rise like a pressure on my chest and the little hairs on my arm and the back of my neck stood on end. I could see energy bleeding out of her green eyes, lighting them like twin emerald stars as energy crackled down her arm, arcing from stud to stud on her armor. It traveled into her sword and it started to glow red hot in her hand.

Then she looked over to me and winked again and slammed her sword into the receiving socket. It was like energy just cascaded into the ground, and I felt like I had dropped down three feet. Nobody else seemed to notice any of this. The motors began to turn, the huge iron gates groaned then started to rise and she withdrew her sword and slid it into her scabbard.

The steward was speaking loudly. "The gates close at seven this evening. If you are not in the gates of the keep by the seventh strike of the bells, you must seek your own shelter for the night." As he spoke, the returning knights passed the day patrol. They saluted each other, my eyes were glued to Lady Celeste and she turned back in her saddle as she went out on patrol and I swear she looked directly at me.

I was cuffed on my ear roughly by the steward again. "Are you listening Herder? I told you to start moving three times."

Oh, I had sort of tuned him out. "Sorry sir." I grabbed the handles of my cart and headed out the gates, looking up to the iron gates suspended in the soaring arch above us. I turned east toward the mountains as soon as I was out. I had found a great rock outcropping just a couple miles away that had brought me luck so far.

I made sure to take a circuitous route through the Whispering Forest, mindful of other scavengers that had their eyes on me. They were probably wondering where I was finding so many relics from the Before. When I was certain I was not being followed, I turned back toward Beggar's Creek and Hawktail River that ran through the keep. They emptied into Dragontooth Lake at the west side of the village.

I grinned, this was going to be so much fun!

Made in the USA
Las Vegas, NV
20 February 2022